FAR-FLUNG
CONTINUUM 1 and 2:

"*A Truly New Type of Anthology* . . . a long time coming and quite unexpected, this title is a real treat to every science fiction fan."

The News American—Baltimore

"The writers are top flight. . . . Can't wait to see what happens!"

Fresno Bee, Fresno, California

"A wide variety of themes and styles that maintain reader interest; and the writing, by veteran sf authors . . . consistently high quality."

Library Journal

"As with the first volume, each story can stand alone. . . . all are very good, varied in technique and scope, and fine examples of great science fiction."

Columbus Dispatch, Columbus, Ohio

"Here are some of the most solid names in current science fiction."

Herald American—Palm Springs

PRAISE FOR

In the CONTINUUM Series

CONTINUUM 1

CONTINUUM 2

Edited by Roger Elwood

A BERKLEY MEDALLION BOOK
published by
BERKLEY PUBLISHING CORPORATION

Copyright © 1974, by Roger Elwood

All rights reserved

Published by arrangement with the author.

All rights reserved which includes the right
to reproduce this book or portions thereof in
any form whatsoever. For information address

Berkley Publishing Corporation
200 Madison Avenue
New York, New York 10016

Library of Congress Catalog Card Number: 73-87184

SBN 425-02864-X

BERKLEY MEDALLION BOOKS are published by
Berkley Publishing Corporation
200 Madison Avenue
New York, N.Y. 10016

BERKLEY MEDALLION BOOKS ® TM 757,375

Printed in the United States of America

Berkley Medallion Edition, JUNE, 1975

Contents

INTRODUCTION

THE first four *Continuum* anthologies are completed. *Continuum 1* contained eight stories, each a series opener by a prominent author; this second volume, the third and the fourth will each also contain eight stories—altogether there is to be a total of 32 stories divided into eight series with four stories per series. For example: Anne McCaffrey's series chronicles the life and career of Killashandra, the Crystal Singer: the first story is entitled, "Prelude to a Crystal Song"; the second: "Crystal Singer"; the third: "Milekey Mountain"; the fourth: "Coda and Finale." Anne's agent, Virginia Kidd, and I feel that these stories are among the finest that Anne has done to date. Another example: Chad Oliver's "Caravans Unlimited" series is concerned with essentially the same protagonists and the same central theme—an inter-galactic trading company that gets involved with the internal affairs of alien races. The first story is entitled "Shaka"; the second: "Stability"; the third: "The Middle Man"; and the fourth: "Monitor." While Anne's stories are decidedly offbeat and poetic in style, Chad's are traditional and rugged; each *Continuum* book will contain another story in the "Caravans" series.

Since these two are examples of series with the same protagonists throughout, it might be appropriate to tell a little about another type of series featured in *Continuum*: the one contributed by Edgar Pangborn. His stories have no characters which continue from one to another but all take place in the same world as did his novel, *Davy*; you might call them pages from the history of that world; the time span might be hundreds of years but the origin is the same. The Pangborn stories are entitled: "The Children's Crusade"; "The Legend of Hombas"; "The Witches of Nupal"; and "Mam Sola's House."

There are five other series, each written by the same author: "Stations of the Nightmare" by Philip José Farmer; a series by Poul Anderson which is, in effect, a continuation of his "Orbit Unlimited" novel of a few years ago—the stories are entitled: "My Own, My Native Land"; "Passing the Love of Women"; "A Fair Exchange"; and "To Promote the General Welfare." As well as: "The Armageddon Tapes" by Thomas N. Scortia; a series of short-shorts by Gene Wolfe, "The Notework of Dr. Stein"; and "Thag."

The final series in the *Continuum* anthologies is one built around the revolving authorship concept. Dean Koontz laid the groundwork for this series, developed the territory into which other authors would venture, and wrote the first story himself; it's entitled "Night of the Storm." Then four other authors wrote the successive stories: "Fire Fountain" by Gail Kimberly" (in this volume); "Darkness of Day" by George Zebrowski and Pamela Sargent; and "Making the Connection" by Barry N. Malzberg.

A total of more than 260,000 words has been devoted to the four *Continuum* anthologies. All of us feel a strong degree of excitement about these books. While maintaining the quality orientation of past all-original anthology series, this group adds another facet: the series concept which links all four tightly together. However, each story remains a separate entity; each can be read and enjoyed by itself without the reader's being cheated in any way. Buy one; buy all four—they stand by themselves *and* they form a continuous narrative over four books and the hundreds of thousands of words.

Roger Elwood

Philip José Farmer

STATIONS
OF THE NIGHTMARE

Part Two: THE STARTOUCHED

1.

THE iron door with the monocle window swung inward. A small cage was shoved in, and a chain connected to it was pulled. The door of the cage rose. A large brown-gray male rat dashed out. The big door closed swiftly and silently.

The windowless room was ten by eight by twelve feet. Its white plaster walls were bare. A closed-circuit TV camera squatted on a bracket at the juncture of a wall and the ceiling. It pointed down at the only furniture: a bed, a chair, and a metal cabinet. The narrow bed held a man. Eyes closed, he lay on his back, his arms by his side, his feet pointing straight up. He was five feet six inches long, broad-shouldered, narrow-waisted, and slim. He was fifty-four years old and had brown hair untouched by gray, a high forehead, bushy brown eyebrows, a thick military-type mustache, and a chin like a ball, deeply indented in its middle. He wore only a hospital gown, His right arm and his left leg were chained to the metal frame of the bed.

The rat ran around the room, sniffing at the base of the walls, then clawed up the sheets of the bed to the man's left foot. It sniffed at the shackle around the ankle and began gnawing at the thick creamy stuff smeared on the shackle.

The cheese, mixed with flecks of crabmeat, disappeared rapidly. The rat touched the man's leg several times with its nose as if searching for more food. The man did not move his leg; his eyelids remained closed.

The rat ran along the man's leg and stopped on the man's stomach. When still the man did not move, the rat crept forward slowly, its nose twitching. It sprang forward at the daub of cheese mixed with meat on the man's face.

The rat never got to the face. It slumped and rolled off the man's body and fell by his neck. Its open mouth revealed that its teeth had been pulled.

The man behind the door turned pale, and he swore. He beckoned to a figure standing at the far end of the hall. A nurse, clothed from head to foot in white coveralls and gloves and a hood with a glass face mask, hurried to him. "Get the rat!" he said.

The nurse gave him a strange look and went inside. With gloved hands, she picked up the dead rat and put it into the cage and came back out of the room. The man locked the door and put the key in the pocket of his white laboratory coat.

"Take it to the lab."

He looked inside the room. The man in the bed had not moved. But it was evident to the watcher that something in the man had detected the danger and taken appropriate measures. And yet it was all impossible.

2.

Leo Queequeg Tincrowdor, looking scared, came out of the woods. He had gone over almost every foot of the area. There were thorn tangles only rabbits could penetrate, and he had scratched his face and hands trying to get into them. His boots were wet for he had waded across the creek that bisected the woods, and mud streaked the sides of his jacket and pants. He had slipped while reaching for a branch to pull himself up a steep bank.

Of the yellow stuff that Eyre had reported, Tincrowdor had seen nothing. But the thing that had turned him pale and made him want to run out of the trees was the impression in the mud even the recent heavy rains had failed to obliterate. It looked innocuous enough. It was only an indentation of some hemispherical object that had been set upon a patch free of grass.

Eyre had told of seeing the thing in a dream, but Tincrowdor was convinced that Eyre was reporting an actual occurrence. He had driven down to the farm where Eyre had been hunting, and had heard the farmer's story of how Riley, Eyre's pointer, had run up onto the porch of the house and cowered under the glider. The farmer had not noticed the dog until he came home for lunch, when his wife told him of seeing the dog run panic-stricken across the fields toward the house. She thought that something had happened to Paul Eyre, but then she saw him standing near the edge of the woods. He seemed all right, so she supposed that the dog had lost its nerve over something and that Eyre would explain when he returned from his quail hunting. Eyre went into the woods and did not come out for several hours. When he did he tried to drag the dog out from under the glider. It leaped for Eyre's face and bit his hand, which Eyre had thrust in front of his face. Eyre tossed the dog over the porch railing and then, as it came after him again, killed it with a charge from his shotgun.

When Eyre told Tincrowdor about the dog, he had professed ignorance about why it had attacked him. Eyre had come home, slept for awhile, or so he said, and had had a strange dream about his hunting of that morning. In the dream, Riley had flushed out two quail, and Eyre had shot at the lead bird. Even as he fired, he realized that it was not a quail but a flying saucer about two feet in diameter. The thing had been hit by the pellets from Eyre's gun and had descended into the woods. Eyre had gone after it but at the edge of the woods had encountered a yellow mist. Some of the mist had coagulated into drops, like a golden-colored mercury.

Then, in his dream, he had seen the saucer drop from a tree onto the ground. He had followed it, had seen the rear parts of a lioness disappear into the bush, and a few moments later, the head and shoulders of a naked woman. She was the loveliest woman he had ever seen.

The following Monday morning, while driving to work, Eyre had suddenly pulled his car over to the side of the road. Fellow workers in a car behind his had investigated and found him in a complete mental withdrawal. Mavice, his wife, had had him taken to a nearby private sanitarium. His condition was diagnosed as catatonia originating from causes unknown.

Tincrowdor and Eyre's son, Roger, had searched through the cornfield along the road where Eyre had stopped his car. They had found some paw prints that Roger, a zoology student, said were those of a large feline, a lion's or a tiger's. The big cat must have had wings, because its prints appeared suddenly between some rows about twenty yards inside the field and disappeared as suddenly about twenty feet deeper inside the field.

Tincrowdor had then gone to the sanitarium, where his friend and poker partner, Dr. Jack Croker, had shown him and Morna Tincrowdor some slides of Eyre's blood.

Four days later, Tincrowdor had decided that he would check out the woods in which Eyre had hunted. Now he knew that Eyre had been reporting, under the guise of a dream, reality.

Tincrowdor was a writer of science fiction, and as such he should have been pleased. A wounded flying saucer, golden haze flowing from the wound, a lovely sphinx, and strange yellow brick-shaped organisms in the tissues of the man who had hunted the saucer and the sphinx. These were the stuff of which science-fiction dreams were made.

Tincrowdor did not looked pleased. He looked terrified.

3.

Paul Eyre had been dreaming of a glittering green city at the far end of an enormous field of red flowers. His eyes opened. He had felt happy until then. He sat up, shocked. He remembered seeing the woman's face among the stalks of corn, the glimpse of the great tawny body beneath her torso, and his foot on the brake pedal. The car had slid to a stop on the soft shoulder of the road. He had put the gear into park and stared at her. She had smiled and waved a white arm at him. Her teeth were not human; they were sharp and widely separated, like a cat's, though they were even. He had begun shaking, and then he had fainted.

And here he was in a strange and bare room.

He started to get off the bed and became aware that an arm and leg were chained to the bed. "Hey, what's going on here?" he yelled. "What's going on?"

His ears drummed, and his heart jumped. He lay down again and stared at the single bright light, a bulb in the ceiling shielded by heavy wires. Then he saw the TV camera, like a one-eyed gargoyle squatting on a metal ledge. A few minutes later, the door opened. A woman shrouded in white cloth and glass entered. In one gloved hand, she held a hypodermic syringe.

The momentarily opened door had revealed, in the hall, a broad and heavy male face with thick black eyebrows, a broken nose, and thick lips.

"How are you, Mr. Eyre?" a muffled voice said from behind the glass plate. She stood at the foot of the bed as if she were waiting for permission to advance.

"Where am I? What's going on?"

"You're in the Adler Sanitarium. You've been in a catatonic state for four days. I'm Mrs. Epples, and I'm here to help you get well. I'd like to give you a shot. It's just to tranquilize you; it won't hurt you"

She was speaking so strangely, so unlike a nurse, he realized, because she was afraid of him. If he said no, she wasn't going to insist.

He felt weak, and his stomach rumbled. He was hungry and weak. His mouth felt as dry as an ostrich's feather.

"I don't want any shot," he said, "so forget it. Why am I chained to this bed? What are you doing in that getup? Do I have some disease?"

The woman looked up at the cold eye of the TV camera as if she expected to get some reassurance from it.

"So many questions at once," she said, and she laughed nervously. "Your're chained to keep you from hurting yourself. We don't know if you have a disease or not, but your blood picture is strange. Until we know what those, uh, organisms are, we have to keep you in quarantine."

"My left arm and right leg are not chained," he said. "So what's to keep me from using them to hurt myself, if that's really what you're worried about? And what organisms are you talking about?"

"They're unknown," she said, ignoring his first comment.

"What if I have to relieve myself?"

"There's a bedpan and toilet paper on the shelf in the stand." she said. "You can reach it."

"And how do I call you to take the pan away?"

"We'll know when you need someone," she said, glancing at the TV camera.

"You mean that someone'll be *watching* me?"

She shrank back, and said, "We don't want you to hurt yourself."

"You have no right to keep me here!" he shouted. "I want out! Now!"

"I'll bring you your food," she said, and she left.

Eyre's rage moved along the spectrum from red to blue. He became frightened and confused. If he had awakened in a strait jacket, and the nurse had told him he had been crazy, he would have understood that. But everything in his situation was *wrong*. He was being held prisoner and lied to. He had no doubt that he was here because of what had happened in the woods —when?—five days ago. And the woman, Mrs. Epples, was afraid of him for some reason. Yet, he was supposed to have lain here in a—what was it?—a cata-something or other? Like a coma? What could he have done to scare her so? Or, was she telling the truth about his blood having some sort of strange germs?

All his life, he had been unable to just sit still and think unless he was figuring out some mechanical device. And then he needed paper and pencil to work out his ideas. He read only the newspapers and journals dealing with hunting or cars or motorboats, or technical books concerned with his type of work.

He could sit for an hour or so watching TV or talking to friends, but then he became restless and had to be up and doing.

Or, perhaps not so much doing, he thought, as moving. He had to keep moving. Why?

It was the first time in his life he had ever asked himself that question. The first time he had asked himself anything about himself. And why was that?

It didn't take many brains to see that his feelings—Tincrowdor would say, his sensitivity—had been sharpened. Nor did it take much intelligence to connect this sharpening with the incident in the wood. Which might mean that the organisms in his blood were responsible. Which meant that they were beneficial. Or did it? Paul Eyre did not really like having improved insight. He was like a man who had spent his whole life building an impregnable castle only to find out that he himself was breaking down its walls.

This analogy made him even more ill at ease. He wasn't used to thinking in nonmechanical terms.

He took refuge in logic. If the organisms had caused changes in him of which he was aware, they had also caused changes of which he knew nothing. Otherwise, why would he be isolated and why would the nurse be so scared of him?

While he was pondering this, he fell asleep. When he awoke, he felt sure that he had been drugged. There were needle marks on his left arm, so many that he must have had some of them when he had first awakened. But he had been so disturbed then that he had not noticed them. Some of them, though, must have come from intravenous feeding. While he slept, he was nourished on a liquid diet.

What had made him drop off so suddenly? He looked around and presently found what he knew he would find. There was, in the shadow cast by the TV, the opening of a small pipe. An anesthetic gas had been expelled into the room to make him unconscious, and the nurse had come in after the gas had been dispelled and had given him a shot and set up the I.V. apparatus.

The gas alone was enough to keep him from escaping. They must really fear him if they thought he also had to be chained to the bed.

His feelings were not limited to fear and rage. Such

precautions also made him feel important. And this was the first time in his life that he had felt, deep down, that he was of any significance to anybody.

He sat up and tested his strength against the chains. He was weak, but even if he had had his full power, he could not come near breaking the steel links. And even if he could, whoever was watching him through the TV would release the gas.

He lay down again and contemplated his situation. It was like life; you couldn't leave it until you died.

4.

Dr. Jack Croker and Leo Tincrowdor sat in Croker's office tearing each other and themselves apart.

"Mavice says that if you don't let her see Paul, she'll get him out of here," Tincrowdor said.

"She'd just be upset if she saw him," Croker said. "And I don't think it'd be wise for her to get anywhere near him. You know why. So why don't you talk her into leaving him in my care?"

"I can't tell her why it's so vital that he be isolated," Tincrowdor said. "And if she's not told, she won't see any reason not to move him elsewhere. Besides, what solid proof do you have that he is dangerous? None, none at all."

Croker could think of evidence. He regretted now telling Tincrowdor anything at all.

"What else has happened?" Tincrowdor said.

"What do you mean?" Croker said. He lit a cigarette to give himself time to think.

"You told me that your lab tech's face was badly scarred from adolescent acne. But after she took blood from Eyre, her face miraculously cleared up. And you said that Backers, a male nurse, had a heart attack while he was in the room with Paul. You were thinking of firing Backers because of his brutality, and you suspected that he was doing something to Paul when the heart attack occurred. It's obvious to anyone with imagination that you believe that those alien organisms have changed Paul, have given him strange powers. And it's obvious that you fear that those organisms might be infectious."

Croker bit his lip. If he told Tincrowdor that the organisms had disappeared, or at least were no longer detectible, then he would have lost one more reason for keeping Eyre. But he was not sure that they had all been excreted. There might be some in tissues unavailable until Eyre died. In his brain, for instance.

"We've collected about two million of the yellow creatures in his urine and fecal matter," he said. "Boiling them in hot water doesn't kill them nor does depriving them of oxygen. About the only way they can be quickly destroyed is through burning. And that takes a minimum temperature of 1500 degrees Fahrenheit. It takes hours for the strongest acids to eat through the coating."

Tincrowdor said, "That alone should make you think they're of extraterrestrial origin."

He regretted saying this immediately. He hadn't told Croker about the paw print in the cornfield or the saucer print in the woods. If Croker really thought the yellow-brick things were from outer space, then he would be adamant about not releasing Eyre.

Nor could Tincrowdor blame him. Paul Eyre free could be a calamity, perhaps extinction, for humanity. But Eyre was a human being with certain inalienable rights. Never mind that most of his fellow Americans professed to believe the same but acted as if they didn't. He believed.

Still, he didn't want to die, along with everybody else, if Eyre really were a danger.

Yet, there were times in the velvet hours of the night, and the clanging minutes of noon, when he wondered if it wouldn't be a good thing if humanity were wiped out. For their own good, of course. Human beings suffered much, some more than others, but they all suffered. Death would put an end to their pain. It would also prevent the birth of more babies whose main inheritance would be pain. Tincrowdor had an obsession about babies. They were born good, he believed, though they had potentialities for evil. Society invariably insisted that they should grow up good, but provided the best and the most fertilizer for evil.

Croker, like most doctors, thought that this was the best of all possible worlds, which was to be expected. Their world gave doctors great respect and prestige and much wealth. It was natural for them to become angry with anything or anybody that might change things as they were. Yet, outside of the very poor, criminals, and policemen, they saw more of evil than anybody. But they fought against anything that might soften evil, just as they had fought against medical insurance until they suddenly saw that a good thing could be made out of it.

Croker was not, however, a typical specimen of his profession. He had some imagination. Otherwise he could not have been a member of the Baker Street Irregulars, the society that proceeds on the premise that Sherlock Holmes was a living person.

It was this imagination that made Croker connect things that his duller colleagues would have seen as entirely disparate. This same gift made him a danger to Eyre.

Tincrowdor was aware that Croker was aware and that Croker, like himself, was being stretched like a piece of bubble gum between his conscience and his duty. Or perhaps, Tincrowdor thought, they were each bubbles being blown up by the situation. If they didn't act soon, they would pop.

And the trouble with me, thought Tincrowdor, is that I'm not really concerned with Paul Eyre as an individual human being. I don't even like Eyre. He'd be better off dead and so would his family. But then, come to think of it, so would I. So why am I interfering? Especially when logic says that the fate of one miserable human being is nothing compared to that of the fate of all humanity.

For one thing, if Eyre were done away with, the case might be closed forever. That this might break off forever any contact with extraterrestrials alarmed him. Besides, like most science-fiction writers, he secretly hoped for vast cataclysms, end-of-the-world invasions from outer space, anything that would polish off most of mankind. Among the survivors would be himself, of course. And this little band, having learned its lesson, would then make a paradise of earth.

In his more light-filled moments he laughed at this fantasy. The survivors wouldn't do a bit better than their predecessors.

Croker, who had been silent, said, "How about a drink, Leo?"

"Drink dims the conscious and illuminates the unconscious," Tincrowdor said, "Yes, I'll have one. Or several."

Croker brought out a fifth of Weller's Special Reserve, and the two silently toasted their thoughts.

Tincrowdor asked for another three fingers and said, "If you murder Eyre, you might have to kill me, too. Not to mention Morna. You wouldn't have enough guts to do that."

"I could kill Eyre and then myself," Croker said cheerfully.

Tincrowdor laughed, but he was taken aback. "You've got too much curiosity to do that," he said. "You'd want to know what those yellow things are and where they came from."

"You'd better tell me all you know," Croker said. "I had thought that the organisms were mutations, though I didn't really believe that."

"You're less hidebound and more perceptive than I thought," Tincrowdor said. "O.K. I'll tell you everything."

Croker listened without interrupting except to request more detailed description of several events. Then he said, "Let me tell you about the rat I released in Eyre's room."

When Croker was finished, Tincrowdor poured himself another drink. Croker looked disapproving but said nothing. He had once shown the writer the brain and liver of a skid-row bum. Tincrowdor had quit drinking for three months. When he started again, he drank as if he were trying to make up for the lost time.

Tincrowdor sat down and said, "Even if Paul isn't carrying a contagious disease, he's a menace. He can kill anything he thinks is dangerous. Or, maybe anytime he gets angry. And he gets angry a lot."

He downed half his drink and said, "So that should make your course of action—and mine—apparent. You can't loose *that* on the world."

"And what will *you* do?" Croker said.

"My God, here are two intelligent and compassionate people discussing murder!" Tincrowdor said.

"I didn't mean that," Croker said. "I was thinking of keeping him locked up, as if he were a sort of Man in the Iron Mask. But I don't know if that is possible. In the first place, a fake death would have to be arranged, but that would lead to almost insuperable complications and connivery. He'd have to seem to have died in a fire, so the body would be unrecognizable. I'd have to supply a body so it'd be a closed-coffin funeral. I couldn't keep him here, because somebody might talk. I'd have to arrange for his transportation elsewhere, and I'd have to pay for his keep. And the first time he got angry or thought he was menaced, he'd kill. And that would cause trouble wherever he'd be."

"And if it all came out, you'd go to jail. And I'd be an accessory before, during, and after the fact. And, to tell you the truth, I don't have the guts to be your accomplice."

"Your only complicity would be your silence, and I'd never say anything about your knowledge of this."

"Why'd you tell me anything in the first place?" Tincrowdor said. "Is it because you wanted someone to share the guilt?"

"Perhaps I thought that if anyone else knew about it, I'd not be able to do anything," Croker said.

"And you could release him with a clear conscience? Your hands'd be tied?"

"Perhaps. But that's out. I can't release him."

He leaned toward Tincrowdor and said, "If his family could be made aware of all the facts, they just might agree to keep him here. It might not be forever, because he may lose this power to kill by thought or however he does it. After all, the organisms have gone. Perhaps the power will, too."

"You don't know his family. Maybe his son and daughter would go along, because they're educated enough and have imagination enough to extrapolate from the situation. But Mavice? Never! She'd think we were crazy with all this talk of flying saucers and yellow stuff and killing by invisible means. The story would be out in no time. She would tell her brothers, who are also umimaginative clods. Not that they'd worry much about Paul. They don't like him. But they'd want to help their sister. She's the baby of their family, and they'd hear about it from her all right.''

''Yeah,'' Croker said. ''How'd you ever get to know the Eyres? They're certainly not the type you'd be friends with.''

''Morna and Mavice were high-school buddies. Mavice stood by Morna when she was being ostracized by her other friends because of some lying story a boy was telling about her. They have been good friends ever since. Despite the disparity in their education and their attitudes—Morna's a liberal, as you know, and Mavice's a flaming reactionary—they manage to get along fine. I had a little affair with Mavice myself, back in the days when I was young and horny and a fine female body meant more to me than a fine female brain.''

''How you ever stood that screeching voice, I'll never understand,'' Croker said. ''But that's neither here nor there. What if Mavice were told a story that doesn't quite fit the facts?''

''I don't know how you could do it and still not be exposed.''

Croker erupted from his chair spilling whiskey over his pants. ''Well, something has to be done and soon!''

There was a knock on the door, and Croker said, ''Who is it?''

''It's Mrs. Epples. May I come in?''

Croker opened the door. Mrs. Epples, looking past him, said, ''I wanted to speak to you alone, Doctor.''

Croker went out into the hall and shut the door. Tincrowdor looked at the fifth and decided not to have any more. A minute later, Croker entered. He looked pale.

''Eyre's dead!''

Tincrowdor opened his mouth, but Croker held up his hand.

''I know what you're thinking, but it's not true, so help me God. Eyre died of natural causes. At least, *I* didn't have anything to do with it.''

5.

Paul Eyre awoke naked on something cold and hard. A scalpel was poised above him and beyond a face, its lower half hidden by a gauze mask. Above the man there glared a hard bright light.

The man's eyes widened, the scalpel jerked away, and he cried, "No! No!"

Eyre rolled off the stone and onto the floor. Though his legs and arms gave way to weakness, he crawled away toward the closed door. Something hard struck the marble floor. The metallic sound was succeeded a second later by the thump of a heavy body.

A few feet from the door, Eyre collapsed. He lay breathing heavily for awhile, knowing somehow that the immediate danger had passed. But out there, beyond the door, and not far away, were other dangers. They were walking up and down the corridors, intent on their business. At least two were thinking about him also.

Their thoughts were neither verbal or iconic. They blew through the door as thin susurruses from two far-off oceans. They lapped around him as the last waves of the sea would roll out on the beach and splash his feet.

As he sat up, he caught another element in the faint whisperings. It identified the sex of the thinkers.

He reached up, grabbed the edge of the stone table, and pulled himself up. Eyre walked around the table, leaning on it, and then got down on his knees to examine the man on the floor. His eyes were open and glazed, his skin was bluish, and he had no pulse. Something, probably a heart attack, had struck him down just as he was about to kill Eyre. But why had he wanted to murder Eyre and to dissect him?

He looked around the room and found nothing with which to clothe himself. The man's clothes wouldn't fit him, but if he had to, he would put them on. He couldn't stay naked. He had to get to a telephone and call the police, but if he went out into the corridor, he'd be seen at once. And there must be others in this plot to kill him. This man wouldn't have been acting alone.

Or would he?

He was confused and weak, from lack of data as well as hunger. And being naked made him feel guilty, as if he had actually committed some crime that had justified the dead man's trying to kill him. First, he'd get some clothes and then he would get out.

He walked slowly to the door and opened it. The corridor was empty except for a very old man shuffling toward him. He wore slippers, pants, a shirt, and an old frayed bathrobe. He was about Eyre's size. His heart beating hard, Eyre waited until the old man was opposite him. He reached out an arm, grabbed the man by his sleeve, and yanked him inside. He disliked using violence on him, yet at the same time he felt angry at him. An image of his own father, aged beyond his years, his mouth hanging open, drooling, passed before him. He hated old people, he realized, and he hated them because they prefigured his own fate.

The hate was good in one way. It gave him the strength to do what was needed. Fortunately, the old man was paralyzed with fright and did not fight. If he had, he might have caused Eyre considerable trouble, Eyre was so weak.

The old man squawked before Eyre could get a hand over the toothless mouth. The door banged shut. The old man rolled his eyes and went limp. Eyre eased him down and began to undress him. At least, the old man didn't stink from lack of bathing. But Eyre couldn't bring himself to put on the stained shorts. Evidently the old man had imperfect control over his bladder.

When Eyre had finished dressing, he looked at the old man, who was still unconscious but breathing. And what would the fellow do when he awoke? He'd arouse everybody, and the hunt would be on. And when Eyre did get hold of the police, what then? Wouldn't the old man be able to charge Eyre with assault and the theft of his clothes? But surely the police would understand the necessity of this.

He had no time to consider the consequences of what he was doing. He had to get out and away.

He put the scalpel in the pocket of the bathrobe and stepped out into the hall. As he walked down the hall, he realized that he was not wearing his glasses. In fact, now that he thought back on it, he hadn't had them when he had awakened in that room. Yet, he had seen perfectly.

This frightened him for a moment but before he reached the end of the hall he felt reassured. Whatever was going on, it wasn't entirely malignant.

At the corner, he thought of stopping to reconnoiter. But it would be better to act as if he belonged here, so he shuffled to his right. He was in another hall, and at once he saw that he should have gone to his left. Ahead of him was a desk behind which sat a nurse, and beyond her another hall at right angles to his. And a man Eyre recognized was walking in it. His profile was that of the apish man Eyre had seen the last time Mrs. Epples had entered the room in which he had been confined.

He repressed the impulse to wheel and go in the opposite direction. A quick movement might attract the man's eye. The male nurse passed on, and Eyre stopped, felt in his pockets as if he had suddenly discovered he'd left something in his room, and then started to turn back. The nurse looked up and saw him.

"What can I do for you?" she said, sharply.

"Nothing," he said. "I forgot my cigarettes."

She stood up and said, "I don't believe I know you. Are you sure you're on the right floor?"

"I was admitted last night," he said and walked away. At the end of the corridor two doors opened onto a balcony. Through their windows he could see across a brightly lit court. He was on the first story.

"Just a minute!" the woman said. "I don't see any new names of the list!"

"Look closer!" he called back and then was trying the handles of the doors. They were locked, and he was not strong enough to break them open with his body. He went on down the hall to his left, ignoring the demands of the nurse that he come back. As soon as he was out of sight, he kicked off the slippers and ran as fast as he could, which was not swiftly, toward the door at its end. It was barred and locked, too. He turned and pushed open the door of the room nearest him and entered. The bed was empty. The door to the bathroom was closed, and inside someone was flushing the toilet. On the bureau near the window were jars and tubes and boxes of ointments and powders.

The windows could be swung open inward, but the bars would prevent anything but air or messages from getting out.

He put his ear to the bathroom door. Despite the rush of water splashing in the washbowl, he could hear the voices in the hall. One was Mrs. Epples'.

"If you do see him, don't go near him, for God's sake!"

"Why not?" a woman said.

"Because he. . .."

The voices trailed off as his pursuers presumably went down the hall to their left.

He opened the door and looked out. Mrs. Epples and another nurse were walking away from him. At the middle of the other hall, the apish male nurse was opening the door to a room. He was working his way down the hall, and soon would be opening the door behind which Eyre stood.

The water was no longer splashing. The woman would be coming out in a minute. He withdrew his head from the hall, tried to estimate the time it would take for the nurse to open the next door, and stepped out into the hall. Another door down the hall was open, and a nurse was looking into the room. Eyre was around the corner and out of sight; the two nurses had disappeared. He was congratulating himself when Mrs. Epples came out of a room four doors from him. He halted, and she screamed.

Before he could go on, she had dodged back into the room and slammed the door. Behind him he heard a shout and the slap of shoes on the floor.

Eyre ran again. There was another shout. He glanced over his shoulder and saw the apish man standing by the corner. Evidently he had no intention of pursuing him any further.

A door opened ahead of him and a thin young man with tousled hair and wild eyes looked out, but when he saw Eyre he shut the door. Eyre opened it and walked in, and the young man cowered against the bed. Eyre did not believe that he was frightened because he knew anything about him. The young man would have been frightened by any stranger.

Eyre said nothing. He went to the closet, opened it, and took out a pair of hush puppies and a jacket. In the bureau drawer he found a wallet and removed a ten-dollar bill, a five, four ones, and some change.

"I'll pay you back later," he said.

The young man shivered and his teeth chattered.

Paul Eyre stepped out of the room just as Mrs. Epples and the apish male nurse came around a corner. They halted, stared at him, and fled.

They were afraid of him, no doubt, but they must have gone for help. However, if everybody was as scared as those two, nobody was going to stop him. Not unless they shot at him from a distance.

Two minutes later, he walked out of the Adler Sanitarium. Only a security guard, a sixty-year-old man, stood between Eyre and freedom. He stepped aside as Eyre approached him because Mrs. Epples was screaming at him from the front entrance.

"Don't use your gun! Let him go! The police will take care of him!"

This startled Eyre. Why would *they* bring in the police? He was the one who had been held prisoner and whom they, or at least some of them, had tried to kill. Or, did they have some good reason for having held him? Was he—he felt cold at the thought—was he carrying some dreadful disease? Had he been infected by that yellow stuff?

If this were so, why hadn't he been told? He would have cooperated to the fullest.

There were about thirty cars in the parking lot. Some of them had unlocked doors, but none of them had keys in the ignition locks. He didn't want to take the time to crosswire one, so he started walking down the road. As soon as he was out of sight of the sanitarium, he turned right into the woods. The Illinois River lay a mile and a half away, and a half mile up its bank was a refuge.

6.

The cottage belonged to a friend who had invited the Eyre family Saturday afternoons for boating and water-skiing and a big meal at night. They would sleep in the two extra rooms, get up for a big breakfast about ten, go to a nearby church, and spend the afternoon on the river. Eyre paid for these weekends by repairing Gardner's boat motors or helping him paint his boats.

The season was over, and the house was shut up. Eyre knew that it held canned foods and blankets. He could hide out there while he tried to find out what was happening to him.

The cottage was about twenty yards from the river and was isolated from the neighboring houses by thick woods on each side. He crouched in the thick bushes behind a big tree while the moon rose.

About two hours after he had hidden, car lights probed down the narrow dirt road leading to the cottage. Shivering, he lay down flat on the cold ground in a little hollow behind the bush. When the lights had passed him, he raised his head. Two cars were parked in the moonlit area before the house. Men in the uniforms of the county police were tramping around the house with flashlights. Presently two went in, and their flashlights speared the darkness within. After ten minutes, the two came out. One of them said, "There's no sign he's been here."

"Yeah, but he might come here later."

One talked over the radio for a minute, then called to the others. "The sheriff said to watch the Y-fork for an hour."

The cars drove away. Eyre stayed where he was. A half-hour later a patrol car, its lights off, rolled into the open area before the house. Two men got out quietly, tried the locks, and cast their flashlight beams through the windows. A few minutes later, they got into the car and drove off.

Eyre waited until three in the morning before entering the house. An extra key was hidden in a stump by the woodpile. Whoever had told the police about this cottage—he suspected Mavice—had forgotten about the key. The moonlight coming in the windows and his knowledge of the place enabled him to locate a bottle of distilled water, a box of powdered milk, and cans of fruit and meat. The water and gas were shut off, so he could not cook, and he had to go outside to relieve himself.

At three thirty, he crawled onto the unsheeted mattress under a pile of blankets. He fell asleep at once but dreamed of flying saucers, yellow bricks, and a green city far off across a red field. He felt a great longing for the city, an overwhelming homesickness. He awoke with the tears only half-dried.

7.

Half an hour after dawn, carrying two blankets, a can that he had filled with water, two opened cans of food, and a sack of garbage, he went back to his hiding place. He fell asleep. Two hours later he was awakened by noises from the house. A car with two county officers was parked out front. He was glad that he had replaced the key in the stump, for an officer was looking inside the stump. Somebody had recalled that it was there. Was it Mavice who had betrayed him? Or one of the kids? Gardner must have given a key to the police, but somebody in Eyre's family had told the police about the cottage. They would not have known about Gardner otherwise.

An officer came out of the house and called to the other.

"Everything's just as we left it."

Fortunately, they had not counted the blankets.

A moment later, the sound of a motor announced another car. His ear identified it as a Porsche, and thus he was not overly surprised when Tincrowdor drove up. What was he doing here?

Tincrowdor got out and talked to the officers, but they spoke too softly for Eyre to hear what they were saying. Several times, Tincrowdor looked out at the woods, and once he looked directly at Eyre but could not see him, of course. Eyre hoped that he wasn't going to suggest to the police that they search the woods.

The policeman got into the car, and Tincrowdor started toward his. As he passed the stump, he dropped something into its open end.

Eyre waited for a half-hour and went to the stump. The key still dangled on a thick cord from a nail driven into the interior wall. Below it lay an old and frayed wallet. He opened it and found a folded letter in it.

Paul,

I'm taking a chance that you may come here and find this. The police don't know I'm doing this, but if they find this, there's nothing they can do about it. I'm only trying to get you to surrender yourself. But please don't tear this up at this point. Read on, because it is vitally important that you do. And when I say *vitally*, I am not exaggerating. It's vital not only for you but possibly for the world itself that you make yourself available at once for study. Study by scientists.

Roger and I found evidence that you were lying when you said you'd dreamed. We know that it must have been reality but that you were afraid you'd be thought crazy if you reported it as reality. And Croker, poor dead Croker, found evidence that you were infected with a completely unknown organism.

It's evident that these things have made some changes in your body. And in your mind. Mrs. Epples had a very badly scarred face from adolescent acne. The scars disappeared after she assisted in getting you to bed in the sanitarium. A male nurse, Backers, suffered a heart attack when he apparently manhandled you. He is a rather brutal person and was not discharged only because help is hard to get at Adler's. No wonder, considering its very low pay scale.

It's obvious that you have powers that nobody else has ever had. Except in science-fiction stories. Or, possibly, some people in the past have had them—Jesus, Faustus, some others, maybe some so-called witch doctors of so-called primitive peoples.

I wouldn't advise you to try walking on the surface of the Illinois. But you can hurt, you can *kill*, and you can *heal*. I don't mean that you can do this consciously. At least not yet. But when you, or your unconscious, or whatever, feels threatened, it reacts violently. By what means, I don't know. I'd guess, by mental means. Definitions or analyses don't matter just now.

You have powers for good and evil. You struck down Croker in, I presume, a moment of panic. Yet, Croker was not trying to kill you. He thought you were dead. You were kept prisoner in that room, and your unconscious, or whatever, took the only means of getting you out of that room. At least, I'm presuming you didn't do it consciously. Your body became, as far as Croker could tell, dead. But you came out of that fake-death state when you were about to be dissected. And Croker paid the price for trying to keep your *condition* a secret.

It's a good thing I'm squeamish and wasn't present to watch the dissection. I went home and so was spared. The old man whose clothes you took seemed to have had a mild heart attack. Apparently you, or whatever, didn't feel that he was an important threat. He died a few hours later, anyway. His old heart couldn't take the minor injury you gave it.

I'm asking you to turn yourself in, Paul. You should voluntarily allow yourself to be locked up, for awhile, at least. You won't be charged with murder or manslaughter, because you couldn't help the deaths. But if you persist in hiding, in running away, you'll be killing more people, and, eventually, you'll be killed.

At the moment, there is very little evidence that your story is true. Croker hid the slides of your blood and his reports on you. We can't find them. Not yet. But Epples and Backers saw the experiment with the rat. You were in an unconscious state, Paul, but you killed a rat that had been released in your room and tried to bite you. It couldn't because its teeth had been removed. You killed it without moving a muscle.

If you give yourself up, the scientists can test you and they'll have to believe what they see. They won't want to, but they'll have to. And then they'll have to believe that an extraterrestrial of some sort, mechanical or biological, has landed on earth. This knowledge they will have to keep to themselves while a quiet search for the extee is conducted. If the news got out, the panic would be terrible.

I won't lie to you, Paul. If the world found out that you were a possible source of infection, you'd be in grave danger. But that's why you need to be kept in a place that is heavily guarded. While you're running around loose, the news might get out, and every man's hand would be against you.

Why do I take the chance that the police may find this letter and so bring about the very situation I've described? Because the situation demands that I take this chance. You are the most important person in the world, Paul. The most important.

You must give yourself up and let events fall where they may.

You know my phone number. Call me, and I'll make arrangements to meet you and have you given a safe conduct.

Leo

8.

Paul Eyre sat in his daughter Glenda's car in the parking lot of Busiris Central High School. It had taken him three hours to settle down his heart and thoughts. By the end of that time he had half-convinced himself that he was indeed the danger Tincrowdor had said he was. He still did not intend to give himself up; at least, not yet. He had little imagination but the letter had shown him what could happen to him. He might be kept the rest of his life in a hospital room. He might be killed by some fanatic who wanted to rid the world of the threat to it he represented. All the guards and precautions that could be imagined would not be enough to make him safe from determined men.

And yet, he wanted to do his duty. Duty demanded that he sacrifice himself for the sake of the world. He could be a walking bomb a thousand times more fatal than a dozen H-bombs.

He did not really feel that he was. He felt lonely and helpless and very scared. He felt like a leper. He felt self-pity. Why had this horrible thing happened to *him*, of all people? What had he done to deserve it? He wasn't a wicked person. He had his faults, though at the moment he couldn't think of any, but they weren't great enough for him to be singled out for a singular punishment. All he had wanted to do was to keep working at Trackless and on his own little business, to enjoy a beer now and then, to go fishing and hunting, to retire someday and spend his remaining years camping, fishing, and hunting. And work on some gadget that would make him rich and famous.

That was all he wanted.

Now, he thought, he knew what the deer and the rabbits felt like when he had been after them. Not that he regretted shooting them. They were beasts of the field, provided by God for his pleasure and good. He had none of that false sentimentality that permitted some to be horrified by the deaths of gentle-eyed and harmless deer, while they thought nothing of slaughter of gentle-eyed and harmless cattle and sheep for their tables. He didn't see them confining themselves to nuts, carrots, and apples.

Nevertheless, as he had made his way through the woods and the city to this parking lot, he had experienced the same horror that the deer must have experienced.

Busiris, a city of 150,000 population, stretched six miles along the western shores of the Illinois. It also covered the three bluffs inland for a distance of five miles. He had walked through the forests and by the farms and the few industries on its northern side, ascended the bluff through some woods, and walked through the outlying areas. He had to cross some of the major roads, and the closer he got to the high school, the more chance he had of being recognized. But he had shaved off his mustache in the cottage, and he was not wearing his glasses.

Using a screwdriver taken from the cottage, Eyre pried open

the front left window of Glenda's car. Reaching in with the other, he brought up the lock on the inside of the door. A moment later, he had crosswired the car and had the motor running. If he were spotted by a patrol car, he would at least try to get away in her Impala.

Three thirty came. The big building spewed forth students. Over two-thirds of the cars had left the lot when Glenda appeared. She had a beautiful though thin face and long black hair. Yet, she was a pitiful figure. She would have been five feet eight inches tall if her back had been an exclamation mark instead of an interrogative. Her legs seemed as thin as the back of a cigarette package. One leg was several inches shorter than the other. She walked with a motion suggestive of a sick snake.

Glenda was a living reproach to her father, though he had only recently recognized it. He had been disappointed when she was born because he had wanted another son. Girls were useless; they demanded special care, became a worry when they were pubescent, and beyond helping their mothers when they got older, couldn't pay their way in his household. Paul Eyre had, however, determined that his daughter was going to be as much like a boy as possible. He had taught her how to repair cars and outboard motors, to do carpentry and electrical work, and to hunt and fish. At least, when she got married, she wasn't going to be a drag like Mavice. Mavice had refused to learn enough to help him in his business. And when she reluctantly went along on his outdoor trips, she griped about the cooking, the boredom and the discomforts.

When Glenda was ten, she had gone with him and Roger to Wisconsin on a fishing trip. She had not been feeling well for several days and had objected to going. Mavice had objected, too. He had stormed at both of them until they subsided. On reaching the little lake, Glenda had become too sick to leave the tent. Eyre had ignored all except her most basic demands and had, in fact, been angry because he thought she was malingering. The second day, Glenda had a high fever and was only conscious now and then. Finally realizing the seriousness of the situation, he had bundled her into a car and driven all night back to Busiris.

Glenda had almost died of infantile paralysis. And she would always be a cripple.

She had never said anything to him about his forcing her to go on the trip. Mavice, however, had more than made up for Glenda's silence. How many times, when they were quarreling, had Mavice thrown this up to him?

Now, watching her hobble bent-backed across the lot, he felt sick. And he understood why her mere presence had made him so angry, why he had longed for the day she would go off to college. Deep down, he knew that it was his selfishness and stupidity that had wrecked her. He had refused to admit that knowledge to his consciousness, but it had nevertheless disturbed him.

He also saw for the first time that Mavice was to blame, too. Why hadn't she held out against him? No matter how he had ranted, she should have refused to let him take an obviously sick child on such a trip.

Both of them were guilty. Both had refused to admit their guilt. The only difference now was that Mavice was still blind, and something had suddenly and painfully opened his eyes.

He knew what that something was. The strange organisms in his body had worked a change in him.

9.

Glenda, seeing him in the driver's seat, stopped. Her pale face became even whiter. Then she came around the side of the car and got in beside him. Tears ran down her cheek.

"What are you doing here, Dad?"

He refrained from telling her that she was his second choice. Busiris College was too far away and too well patrolled for him to try to see Roger.

He told her all that had happened and described Tincrowdor's letter, Glenda looked stunned.

"I didn't want to phone Leo because the police might've

tapped his wires," he said. "I want you to get to his house and arrange for him to be in the phone booth near the downtown public library. I'll call him from another booth."

"I just can't believe all this!" Glenda said. "It's too fantastic!"

"I'm not crazy, and Leo will tell you so," he said. "The world has enough problems, more than it can handle, as everybody, including God, knows. But now, in the past few days, it has two new problems. And both make all past problems look simple. One is that saucer creature. The other is me. I can turn myself in and give the world a chance to solve the dilemma I represent. But what's going to prevent the saucer thing from infecting other people? Nothing, nobody, is going to be able to do anything about that. Except me."

"What do you mean?" she said. She leaned over and placed a hand on his arm. He moved it away, feeling that he might be contagious.

"I mean that there's something of the saucer thing in me. It's changed me, is still changing me. I'm part saucer thing myself. Otherwise, why would I have those dreams of that green city and the longing for it? You see before you a man who's still your father but not your father. Half-human. Or, maybe I was only half-human before and it's making me more human. I don't know. Anyway, it takes a thief to catch a thief, and I'm the only one who can catch the saucer thing. That's because I'm part saucer thing, and the saucer thing herself is dogging me. Why, I don't know. There's so much I don't know. But I'm convinced that only I can trap her. Which is why I'm not going to turn myself in. But I need help to stay out of the hands of the police. That's why I want to talk to Tincrowder. Maybe he'll help me."

"Dad," Glenda said in a choked voice. "I'm sick!"

She fell against him, and even through his shirt he could feel the heat from her face. He pushed her back so that she sat up as straight as she ever would be able to. Her head hung forward, mouth open; she breathed as if a rusty windmill was in her throat.

"I'm not *angry* with you, Glenda!" he cried. "My God, I love you!"

10.

Once, he had deserted her when she had been sick. There had been no excuse then for what he had done. Now, if he deserted her, he would have an excuse. He couldn't let himself be caught. And logic certainly told him to leave her. He could phone in to the hospital and then take off. Glenda would be taken care of, and he would be safe.

He thought for sixty seconds or so and then drove out of the lot and headed toward the Methodist Hospital. Glenda probably needed to get to a hospital as swiftly as possible, and he would not be responsible for even a second's delay.

He drove as fast as he could, passing three stop signs and two red lights. His car pulled up at the emergency entrance four minutes later. After running inside and telling the nurse at the admittance desk, he went to the public phone down the hall. He dialed his home number but hung up after the phone had rung twenty times. Then he dialed Tincrowdor's number. Morna answered.

He told her to shut up and listen while he explained the situation.

"You get Mavice and Roger down here and take care of things," he said, "And tell Leo I'll be getting in touch with him. 'Bye!"

He walked down the hall away from the emergency room. He heard the nurse calling after him but did not look back. A minute later, he went out by the main exit, past the policeman standing guard there. He strode up the slope along the hospital, cut over to a side street that led to Main Street, and took a bus. Two blocks from his house, he got off at Sheridan and Lux. He phoned the hospital and asked for Mavice Eyre, the mother of the girl who had just been brought in. He waited for two minutes before Mavice answered, then hung up and walked to his house, hoping that Roger would not be there.

He saw no one who knew him until he got to his house. Across the street was the three-storied nursing home filled with old people who had often seen him come and go and watched him when he worked on cars and boats in his driveway. About eight of them, mostly old ladies, were sunning themselves on the side porch as he went up the driveway to the rear of his house. They looked curiously at him but none waved. Apparently, his strange clothes and lack of spectacles and mustache had deceived them.

Under a washbowl on a stand by the rear door was a key. Fifteen munutes later, he left his house. He was dressed in his own clothes and carried a wallet with fifty dollars, and a shotgun and thirty shells. He got into Roger's car; its motor was still warm. Evidently Roger had gotten home just in time to drive his mother to the hospital in her car.

Paul Eyre had no specific place in mind to go to. He would drive out of the city, abandon the car, and walk to one of the riverside cottages deserted for the season. There he would wait as long as he was left alone.

It didn't matter where he was. Sooner or later, the saucer thing in its saucer form, or in that of the sphinx, would show up. And then he would destroy it. Or, it would destroy him.

As he got to the end of his street, he saw a patrol car pull across it, blocking his car. He slammed on the brakes, backed with a squeal of tires into a driveway, and raced away. The rear-view mirror showed him the police car backing up so it could swing around.

When he looked again, he saw another black-and-white car, its red lights flashing, pull around the corner ahead of him.

He put the car into neutral, opened the door, and fell out of it while it was still moving. He ran for the old folks' home, the sanctuary of senior citizens, the elephants' graveyard. The old ladies on the front porch screamed. One stood in his path. Rage flashed through him. The woman fell on her face. Shouts of male voices tore at him, and as he went through the door into a huge dining room, he heard a shot. A warning fired into the air.

He crossed a big room into a smaller one, went past that through a kitchen, and out the door. He vaulted over a fence with an agility he did not know he possessed. But he had forgotten about the savage police dog the Hunters kept. Though it was chained, it had enough leash to get at him. It sprang at him and dropped upon the ground and lay still, its tongue hanging out, its eyes glazing.

He stopped and turned toward the big house, his arms up in the air. If he kept on running, he would kill half the world, and he could not endure that thought. He would surrender now, and if the police shot him because they were afraid to let him stay alive, so much the better. That would solve many problems.

The police, of course, did not shoot. They had not been told how dangerous he was, nor did they know then that he had left three old women dead behind him. Even if they had, they would have thought that the excitement was too much for the aged hearts.

That is exactly what the few authorities who knew the truth allowed the police and the public to think. He was not brought to trial on any charge but was declared to have been examined by psychiatrists and found insane.

Eyre did not argue with the decision. Nor did he tell his keepers about the incident, three nights after being locked up, when he had awakened and looked out of the window. Outlined in its frame was a saucer shape. It hovered for a few seconds and then flashed upward out of sight. Eyre felt that it—she—was watching over him because he was her only living offspring. Or, something inside him was.

11.

Six months passed without his seeing a human being in the flesh. From time to time he awoke knowing that a gas had put him to sleep and samples of his tissues had been taken from him. Once, he awoke with an x-ray photo on the table beside him. The TV had come to life then, and Dr. Polar's image had told him what the x-ray meant. It was of his brain, and the arrow drawn on it pointed to a tiny spot in his cerebellum, the "hind brain." This was something that had been detected by radioactive tracing. It might be a tumor, but Dr. Polar did not think it was. Its shape was too much like a brick's. Dr. Polar admitted that he would like to operate to extract it. But he was afraid that the surgeon would drop dead before the knife could make its first cut.

"Apparently, *it* doesn't object to our taking tissue samples or doing certain other experiments," Polar said. "These don't threaten you, or it, I should say."

Eyre asked about *its* nature but was told that Polar and his colleagues didn't even have any theories about it. Eyre then asked if Polar planned to kill him so he could dissect him. Polar did not answer.

He also asked a number of times about Glenda. Each time, he was told that she was alive and doing well. That was all he could, or would, be told.

On the first day of the seventh month, as Eyre paced back and forth, the door to his room opened. Glenda walked in, and the door was quickly shut and locked.

Eyre was so overwhelmed that he had to sit down in his chair. Glenda stood tall and straight, her breasts were no longer just little buds, and her legs were even and shapely. She smiled at him and then broke into tears and ran to him. He cried, too, though at one time he would have thought it unmanly to do so.

"I almost died," she said, after she had left his arms. "My bones got soft. The doctors said nothing like this had ever happened before. They said the calcium was semi-dissolved. The bones were like rubber at first and then like a hard jelly. They kept me in a kind of bath-bed; I floated in water while they put braces and molds around me to straighten me out. After a few weeks, the bones began to get hard again. It took two months for them to become completely hard, and it was so long, so very long, and so frightening! But look at me now!"

Eyre was happy for a long time. But when Glenda said that he wasn't going to be freed, he became angry.

"Why not? I can do great good, more good than anybody has ever done before!"

"Dad, they can't let you go. Everytime you got mad at someone, you'd kill him. Besides. . . ."

"Well, what is it?" he said. He hoped he wouldn't be getting angry with her. Maybe he should tell her to get out now.

"We're all in prison here!" she said, and she began to cry.

Though there was no reason to ask why, he did so. The authorities, whoever they were, had locked up not only his family but the two Tincrowdors, Mrs. Epples, and Backers in this place. They were well treated and given everything they wanted except their freedom.

"But what about our friends and relatives?"

"They've been told we are all being treated for a rare contagious disease. I don't know how long they're going to believe that, but I think some sort of indirect pressure is being put on them. They're not to say anything about this to anybody else. We get letters, and we can write letters. But they're censored. We've had to rewrite some of them."

Eyre was in a rage for two days and a funk for three. The sixth day, Dr. Polar appeared on the TV screen. He waited until Eyre had quit storming at him and then said, "It's not as bad as it seems to you, Paul. There may be a way out for all of us. I want you to go to the door now. The view-window will be opened for a minute. I want you to just look through it. That's all."

Since there was no reason to refuse, Eyre did so. He saw only a baby, about a year old, lying on a bed. The baby had a wasted face and very thin arms and legs and was obviously dying. Eyre felt pity for it.

Then the window was slid shut by someone out of his view.

Three days later, the door opened, and Glenda entered. They embraced each other, and Glenda said, "The baby is completely cured, Dad. It had leukemia and would have died in a week or so. Now, it's cured. The doctors won't admit that, but they do admit that there's been a complete remission."

"I'm glad of that," he said. "But what does that mean for me? And for you?" he added hastily. "And the others?"

Glenda gave him an uninterpretable look, and said, "If you'll cooperate, Dad, we'll be set free. We can't tell the truth when we get out, and if we should slip up, we'll be in trouble. But we'll be free. If. . . ."

It was evident that she was ashamed, and yet she longed desperately for him to say yes. Nor could he blame her. She had been set free from her crooked body only to be denied the new life promised her.

"What do the others say?"

"Mom is going to go crazy, literally crazy, Dad, if she can't get out. Roger says the decision is up to you. Morna Tincrowdor says she'll do everything she can to get you out, but she's just talking, and she knows it. Leo Tincrowdor says you're not to give in to the bastards. But then he's happy. He gets all the books and booze he wants and he doesn't have to support himself. He sends a message. 'Stone walls do not a prison make.' I think he means by that you'll get out by yourself, somehow."

"If they wanted me to do something evil," he said, "I'd have to refuse, and I'm sure you wouldn't want me to say yes. But I do say yes. Only, Glenda, promise me you won't forget me. You'll write me at least once a week. And you'll come to see me once in awhile."

"Of course I will, Dad," Glenda said. "But it doesn't seem fair! You have this gift, you'll be doing good for many people, and yet you'll be kept in prison!"

"I won't be the first," he said. "Nor the last. Anyway, they're keeping me here so I won't hurt people, though God knows I don't wish anyone harm. Not consciously, anyway."

He bent close to her and whispered, "Tell Tincrowdor to keep looking. He'll know what I mean."

Late that night, he awoke knowing that someone, or something, was near and wanted him awake. He rose and went to the window and looked out over a wall and a river beyond it and a city sparkling with many lights. Near the window, perhaps twenty feet away, the saucer hung. It was whirling, and its rotation seemed to be making the noise he had heard in his sleep. The humming was modulated, and its message, so it seemed to him, was one of farewell. Farewell and sadness. It had come to earth for some unknown reason, had met with an accident, had caused an unplanned change in another creature, and now must leave. Whatever it had planted in him, it felt that the planting had not and would not come to fruition.

Suddenly, it shot upward. He thrust his face against the bars and looked up but could no longer see it. When he walked away from the window, the vision of the red fields and the green city flashed before him. Was that a vision of the thing's home? Was the vision broadcast to him by some mental means from the thing? Or, did he carry inside himself one of its progeny, and did this child carry inside itself an ancestral memory of the home of its mother? And was it able to transmit this hereditary vision to him now and then, when he, or it, or both, were under some stress?

He would never know now, he told himself. The visitor had come because of mysterious reasons and had left for mysterious reasons. Whatever her mission was, it had been aborted.

It was his fate to be the only human being touched by the stars. And it was his fate that other human beings were afraid of the startouched. So, while the giver of the two-edged gift roamed through the spaces between the stars, he, the recipient, was shut up in one small room. Forever.

"Not forever," he muttered. "You might keep me in if I was just a human being. But I'm more than that now. And you will wish you hadn't locked me up. You'll wish you had treated me like a human being."

Poul Anderson

PASSING THE LOVE
OF WOMEN

AFTER three hours of troubled sleep, Dan Coffin awoke to the
same knowing: *They haven't called in.*

Or, have they? his mind asked, and answered: *Unlikely. I
gave strict orders I be told whenever word came, whatever it
was.*

*So Mary's voice has not reached us since dusk. She's lost, in
danger.* He forced himself to add: *Or, she's dead.*

Forever stilled, that joyousness that ran from the radio to him
especially? "Remember, Dan, we've got a date exactly three
tendays from now. 'Bye till then. I'll be waiting." No!

Understanding it was useless, and thinking that he ought to
get more rest, he left his bunk. The rug, a cerothere hide, felt
scratchy under his bare feet, and the clay floor beyond was cold.
The air did surround him with warmth and sound—trillings,
croakings, the lapping of waves, and once from the woods a
carnivore's scream—but he hardly noticed. Paleness filled the
windows. Otherwise his cabin was dark. He didn't turn on a
light to help him dress. When you spend a lot of time in the
wilderness, you learn how to do things after sunset without a
fluoropanel over your head.

Weariness ached in him, as if his very bones felt the drag of a
fourth again earth's gravity. *But that's nonsense,* he thought.
His entire life had been spent on Rustum. No part of him had
ever known earth—except his chromosomes and the memories

they bore of billionfold years of another evolution—*I'm simply worn out from worrying.*

When he trod outside, a breeze ruffled his hair (as Mary's fingers had done) and its coolness seemed to renew his strength. Or, maybe that came from the odors it brought, fragrances of soil and water and hastening growth. He filled his lungs, leaned back against the rough solidity of walls, and tried to inhale serenity from this, his homeland. A few thousand human beings, isolated on a world that had not bred their race, must needs be wary. Yet, did they sometimes make such a habit of it that there could be no peace for them ever?

The two dozen buildings of the station, not only the log shelters like his own but the newer metal-and-plastic prefabs, seemed a part of the landscape, unless they were simply lost in its immensity. Behind them, pastures and grainfields reached wanly to a towering black wall of forest. Before them, Lake Moondance murmured and sheened to a half-seen horizon; and above that world-edge soared mountains, climbing and climbing until their tiers were lost in the cloud deck.

The middle of heaven was clear, though, as often happened on summer nights. Both satellites were aloft there. Raksh was nearly at maximum distance, a tiny copper sickle, while Sohrab never showed much more than a spark. The light thus came chiefly from natural sky-glow and stars. Those last were more sharp and multitudinous than was usual when you looked up through the thick lowland air. Dan could even pick out Sol among them. Two sister planets glowed bright enough to cast glades on the lake, and Sohrab's image skipped upon it as swiftly as the moonlet flew.

It's almost like a night on High America, Dan thought. The memory of walking beneath upland skies, Mary Lochaber at his side, stabbed him. He hurried toward the radio shack.

No one ordinarily stood watch there, but whoever was on patrol—against catlings, genghis ants, or less foreseeable emergency makers—checked it from time to time to see if any messages had come in. Dan stared at the register dial. Yes! Half an hour ago! His finger stabbed the playback button. "Weather Center calling," said a voice from Anchor. "Hello,

Moondance. Look, we've got indications of a storm front building off the Uranian coast, but we need to check a wider area. Can you take some local readings for us?'' He didn't hear the rest. Sickness rose in his throat.

A footfall pulled him back to here and now. He whirled rather than turned. Startled, Eva Spain stepped from the threshold. For a moment, in the dim illumination of its interior, they confronted each other.

"Oh!" She tried to laugh. "I'm not an urso hunting his dinner, Dan. Honest, I'm not."

"What are you after, then?" he snapped.

If that were Mary, tall and slim, hair like sunlight, standing against the darkness in the door— It was only Eva. In the same coarse coveralls as him, with the same knife and pistol—tools—at her belt, she likewise needed no reduction helmet on her red-tressed, snub-nosed, freckle-faced head. Also like him, she was of stocky build, though she lacked the share of Oriental genes that made his locks dark, cheekbones high, skin tawny. And she had a few years less than he did, whereas Mary was of his age. That didn't matter; they were all young. What mattered was that this was not Mary.

Now, don't blame Eva for that, Dan told himself. *She's good people.* He recalled that for a long while, practically since they met, everybody seemed to take for granted that in due course they would marry. He couldn't ask for a better wife, from a practical viewpoint.

Practicality be damned.

Her eyes, large and green, blinked; he saw light reflected off tears. Yet, she answered him stiffly: "I could inquire the same of you. Except I'd be more polite about it."

Dan swallowed. "I'm sorry. Didn't mean to be rude."

She eased a little, stepped close and patted his hand. Her palm was not as hard as his; she was a biologist, not an explorer who had lately begun farming on the side. Nevertheless he felt callouses left by the gear and animal harness that every lowlander must use.

(Mary's touch was soft. Not that she was an idler. Even on High America, survival required that every healthy adult work, and she did a competent job of keeping the hospital records. But she never had to cut brush, midwife a cow, cook on a wood fire for a campful of loggers, dress an animal she herself had shot and cure its hide. Such was lowlander labor, and it would be death for Highland Mary to try, even as it was death for her to be long marooned in the wilderness around Lake Moondance.)

"Sure," Eva said gently, "I understand. You've fretted your nerves raw."

"What does bring you here at this hour?"

"The same as you." She frowned. "Do you think I'm not concerned? Bill Svoboda and the Lochabers, they're my friends as well as yours."

Dan struck fist in palm, again and again. "What can we *do*?"

"Start a search."

"Yes. One wretched little aircar available, to scout over how many thousands of square kilometers? It'd take days to assemble a fleet of vehicles. They haven't got days. Bill does, maybe, but . . . Mary and Ralph . . . very possibly don't."

"Why not? If their helmets are intact——"

"You haven't seen as many cases as I have. It takes a pretty strong man, with considerable training, to wear one of those rigs almost constantly. When your own chest expansion has to power the reduction pump—the ordinary person can't sleep in one of them. That, and sheer muscular exhaustion, make the body extra vulnerable to pressure intoxication, when the victim takes the helmet off so he can rest."

Dan had spoken in a quick, harsh monotone. Eva replied less grimly: "They can't be any old where. They were homebound, after all."

"But you know they, the Lochabers, they wanted to see more of the countryside, and Bill promised he'd cruise them around. They'd've been zigzagging the whole way. They could have landed at random, as far as we're concerned, for a closer look at something, and come to grief. Even if we pass near, treetops or crags or mists can hide their vehicle from us."

"I'm aware that this is a rather large and not especially mapped country." Eva's response was dry. It broke into anger. She stamped her foot. "Why are you moping around like this?

Dan Coffin, the great discoverer! Won't you *try*?"

He hit back indignation of his own. "I intend to start at dawn. I assure you it's no use flying at night, it's a waste of fuel. Light-amplifier systems lose too much detail, in that complicated viewfield where the smallest trace may be the one that counts. The odds are astronomical against chancing in sight of a beacon fire or in metal-detector range or—" He slumped. "Oh, God, Eva, why am I being sarcastic? You've flown more than I have. It's so huge a territory, that's all. If I had the slightest clue——"

Once more her manner mildened. "Of course." Slowly: "Could we maybe have such a lead? Some faint indication that they might have headed one way rather than another? Did Mary—did Mary tell you she was especially interested in seeing some particular sight?"

"Well, the geysers at Ahriman," he said in his wretchedness. "But the last call-in we got from them was that they'd visited this and were about to proceed elsewhere."

"True. I've played back that tape a few times myself."

"Maybe you put an idea into their heads, Eva? You saw considerable of them, too, while they were here."

"So I did. I chatted about a lot of our natural wonders. Ralph's fascinated by the giant species." She sighed. "I offered to find him a herd of terasaur. We flew to Ironwood where one had been reported, but it had moved on northward, the trail was clear but there was a thunderstorm ahead. I had trouble convincing Ralph how foolish we'd be to fly near that weather. Just because lowland air currents are slow, those High Americans always seem to think they lack force. . . . No, Ralph's bright, he knows better; but he does have a reckless streak. Why am I rambling? We——"

She broke off. Dan had stiffened where he stood. "What is it?" she whispered.

"That could be the clue we need." The night wind boomed under his words.

"What?" She seized him by the wrist. Only afterward did he notice that her nails had broken his skin.

"Terasaur—they migrate upward in summer, you know. Bill

could've promised to locate a herd for the Lochabers, maybe the same herd you failed to see. Their tracks are easy enough to spot from above——'' He grabbed her to him. "You're wonderful! It may turn out to be a false lead, but right now it is a lead and that's plenty. Come daybreak, I'm on my way!"

Tears broke from her, though her voice stayed level. "I'm coming along. You may need help."

"What? I'll take a partner, certainly——"

"The partner will be me. I can pilot a car, shoot a gun, or treat an injury as well as anybody else. And haven't I earned the right?"

In the several years of his career as an explorer, Dan Coffin had often returned to High America. Not only did the scientists and planners want the information he gathered about this planet that they hoped to people with their descendants; but he himself must discuss further expeditions and arrange for equipping them. Moreover, he had family and friends there.

Additionally, at first, he found refreshment of both body and spirit in the land. High America rose above the cloud deck that covered most of Rustum most of the time; its skies were usually clear, its winters knew snow and its summers cool breezes through their warmth. Compared to the low country, it was almost like earth.

Or so he imagined, until gradually he began to wonder. He had gotten a standard teaching about the variations. The sun was smaller in earth's sky though somewhat more intense, its light more yellowish than orangy. Earth took one-point-seven years to complete a circuit around Sol, but spun on its axis in a mere twenty-four hours. There was a single moon, gigantic but sufficiently far off that it showed half the disc that Raksh did and took about eleven days (about thirty earth-days) for a cycle of phases. Dan Coffin, who weighed a hundred kilos here, would weigh eighty on earth. The basic biologies of the two worlds were similar but not identical; for instance, leaves yonder were pure green, no blue tinge in their color, and never brown or yellow except when dying. . . .

Searching his memories, then asking questions carefully

framed, he came to realize how poorly the older people—even those who had grown to adulthood on earth, and even when helped by books and films—were able to convey to him some sense of what the mother globe really was like. Did the differences add up to such alienness that they themselves could no longer quite imagine it? And if this was true, what about the younger folk, the Rustumites born? And what about the children whom they in turn were starting to have?

So did Dan Coffin really need High America?

Most humans absolutely did, of course. The air pressure at lower altitudes was too much for them, made them ill if they were exposed more than very briefly, eventually killed them. But his body could take it, actually thrive on it. In fact, on each return he missed more keenly the high-metabolism vigor that was his down below, the clarity of sound and richness of smells. Besides, High America was too damn cramped. Oh, there was still a lot of fallow real estate; but the future belonged to those who could settle the lowlands. Already the whole wild, beautiful, mysterious, limitlessly beckoning surface of the world was theirs.

He continued to enjoy his visits as a change of pace, a chance to meet people, savor the civilized amenities, roister a bit in what few establishments Anchor supported for that purpose. Yet, it was always good to get back to Moondance. This became especially true after Eva Spain arrived there.

Like him, she had been an exogenetic baby, her parentage selected with a view to tolerance of dense air. The result was equally satisfactory for her. He and she could both descend to sea level in comfort, which made them natural partners. Most of those who were beginning to settle the lowlands did not care to go that far down; Moondance station was at two kilometers altitude. Eventually, man as a whole would be able to live anywhere on the planet. That evolution wouldn't take a dreadfully long time, either: because the few who *now* had full freedom were sure to have a disproportionate share in the heredity.

Dan and Eva . . . they worked well together, liked each other, there was no burning romance but there was a growing attraction and certainly a marriage would make excellent sense from every standpoint. But then, for the first time since school days, he encountered Mary Lochaber.

This near-summer solstice, at this middle latitude, daylight would endure for about forty-two hours. The searchers intended to lose none of them. Their aircar was aloft before the first eastward paling of the clouds.

Those had again covered the sky. Dan remembered Mary wondering how he could endure such almost perpetual gloom. "It's not like that at all," he answered. "Still another thing you ought to experience for yourself."

Finally she had come, and—his knuckles stood white on the controls.

Eva turned her eyes from the forest. Beneath silver-bright heaven, in the absence of clear shadows, its treetop hues were an infinitely subtle and changeable intermingling. Their endlessness was broken by the upheaval of a plutonic tor, the flash of a waterfall and a great river, the splendid northward climbing of the entire land. Kilometers away, uncountable birds moved like a storm.

"You really are suffering, aren't you?" she asked quietly.

He heard his own voice, rough and uneven: "I used to revel in the sheer bigness of the country. Now, when we have to find one speck that's gotten lost somewhere, it's horrible."

"Don't let it get to you that way, Dan. Either we learn to live with the fact of death—here—or we can never be happy."

He recalled the tidal cross-chop that had capsized their boat when they were taking biological samples off the Hephaestian coast. Half-stunned, he might have drowned if she hadn't come to his aid. Toshiro Hirayama, who had been like a brother to both of them, was indeed lost. The rest of the crew clung to the keel for hours before a rescue flyer found them. She got back her merriment as fast as any of the others. Nevertheless she still laid a wreath now and then before Toshiro's little cenotaph.

"You're a fine girl, Eva," Dan said.

"Thanks," she answered low. "However, it's another girl on your mind, isn't it?"

"And Ralph. And Bill."

"Mainly her. Right?"

Brought up in his stepfather's tradition that a man should not reveal his private feelings to the world, Dan had to struggle for a moment before he could nod and say: "Yes."

"Well, she is beautiful." Eva spoke without tone. "And a very charming, gracious person. But a wife for you?"

"We . . . hadn't discussed that . . . yet."

"You've been giving it some mighty serious thought. And so has she."

His heart stumbled. "I don't know about her."

"I do. The way her look dwells on you, the voice she speaks in when you are there—it's obvious." Eva bit her lip. "Is either of you in earnest, though? Truly?"

He thought of long talks, of hikes and horseback rides across her father's lands, of dances in Wolfe Hall and afterward walking her home under frosty stars and hasty Sohrab and the bronze light of Raksh upon a clangorous river. There had been kisses, no more; there had been words like, "Hey, you know, I like you," no more. Yet, he had felt that when he came to dinner, her parents (and Ralph, her brother, who shared her blonde good looks and sunny temperament) were studying him with a certain amiable intensity.

She herself? "I'm not sure," he sighed. "They've got such a . . . a different style on High America."

Eva nodded. "It might not count as a decent-sized village on earth," she said, "but Anchor is where most of the population on Rustum centers, and where the industry and wealth and culture are. The alpine hinterland may be sparsely settled, but essentially it's been tamed. People have leisure for fine manners. They may even be overcultivating that kind of thing, as a reaction against the early hardships. Meanwhile we're the raw frontier folk."

"You're hinting at a social gap? No, the Lochabers aren't snobs. Nor are we yokels. We're scientists, carrying out research that is both interesting and necessary."

"Granted. I don't want to exaggerate. Still, it was getting to know those friends of yours—a sort of overnight intimacy that never quite happens in their own safe environment—that drove home to me the fact that there is a difference.''

He could not kiss Mary at Moondance. A glassite bulb sealed off her head, maintaining an air pressure that was normal for her. The same pressure was kept in the station's one small guesthouse; but it took discouragingly long to go through its decompression chamber when one's own lungs were full of lowland atmosphere. Anyway, she shared it with her brother.

But there were rich compensations. At last he could show her something of his world, that overwhelmingly greatest part of the planet she had known only from reading, pictures, a few stereotyped tours, and his words. During five magical days, she and Ralph could wander with him and Eva through the templelike vastness, intricacy, and serenity of the woods, or go ahorseback on a laughing breakneck hunt, or see how biological engineering joined slowly with hard work and patience to make the soil bear fruit for man, or. . . .

Rakshlight glimmered on the curve of her helmet and the long fair tresses within. It made a rocking bridge across the waters, which lapped against the boat louder and more chucklingly clear than ever waves did in the highlands. Wind had died, though coolness still breathed through the summer air, and the sail stood ghostly. That didn't matter. Neither he nor she were in any hurry to return.

She asked him: ''Where does the name Moondance come from?''

''Well,'' he said, ''the lake's big enough to show tides when Raksh is as close as now; and then the reflections gleam and flash around the way you see.''

She caught his hand. ''I was thinking,'' she murmured, ''it ought to be Moon-Dan's. Yours. To me it always will be. What you're doing is so great.''

''Oh, really,'' he stammered, ''I'm just a servant. I mean, the scientists give me instrument packages to plant and collect, experiments and observations to carry out, and I follow orders. That's all.''

"That is not all, as you perfectly well know. You're the one who has to cope and improvise and invent, in the face of unending surprises. Without your kind of people, we'd forever be prisoners on a few narrow mountaintops. How I wish I could be one of you!"

"Me too," he blurted.

Was she suddenly as half-frightened as he? She was quick to ask: "Where did Ralph and Eva go?"

He retreated likewise into the casual. "I'm not sure. Wherever, I'd guess their flit will pass over the Cyrus Valley. She's mighty taken by your car. She's been faunching to try it out under rough conditions. The updrafts there——"

Her tone grew anxious. "Is that safe?"

"Sure, yes. Eva's an expert pilot, qualified to fly any vehicle at any air density. This model of yours can't handle much unlike the H-17, can it? It's only a modification." Because there was around him the splendor of his country, he had to add: "You know, Mary, what worries me is not how well the craft performs, but what its engine may signify. I've read books about what fossil fuels did to the environment on earth; and here you're re-introducing the petroleum burner."

She was briefly taken aback. "Haven't you heard?" A laugh. "I guess not. You seem to have other things on your mind when you visit us. Well, the idea is not to replace the hydrogen engine permanently. But petroleum systems are easier to build, with far fewer man-hours; mainly because of fuel storage, you know. Dad thinks he can manufacture and sell them for the rest of his lifetime. By then, there should be enough industrial plants on Rustum that it'll be feasible to go back to a hydrogen economy. A few hundred oil-fired power plants, operating for thirty or forty years, won't do measurable harm."

"I see. Good. Not that I'm too surprised. Your brother was telling me yesterday about the work he does in his spare time, drilling into children how they must not repeat the old mistakes. . . ." Again he skirted too near the thing that was uppermost in his heart. "Uh, by the way, you mentioned wanting to see more of the lowlands on your way home, if you could get a pilot who can safely take you off the mapped and beaconed route. Well, I may have found one."

She leaned close. Her gaze filled with moonlight. "You, Dan?"

He shook his head ruefully. "No. I wish it were, but I'm afraid I've taken too much time off from work as is. Like Eva. However, Bill Svoboda is about due for a vacation and——"

The three of them had flown away into silence.

Eva's yell cut like a sword. "*There!*"

She swung the car around so the chassis groaned and brought it to hover on autopilot, a hundred meters aloft and jets angled outward. Dan strained against the cabin canopy, flattening his nose till tears blurred vision and he noticed the pain that had brought them forth. His heart slugged.

"They're alive," he uttered. "They don't seem hurt." Mutely, his companion passed him his binoculars. He mastered the shaking of his hands and focused on the survivors below him and the scene around them.

Mountains made a rim of russet-and-buff woods, darkling palisades, around a valley shaped like a wide bowl. Save for isolated trees, it was open ground, its turquoise grass rippling and shimmering in wind. A pool near the middle threw back cloud images. That must have been what first attracted the terasaur.

They numbered some thirty adults, five meters or more of dark-green scaliness from blunt snouts to heavy tails, the barrels of their bodies so thick that they looked merely grotesque until you saw one of them break into a run and felt the earthquake shudder it made. Calves and yearlings accompanied them; further developed than Terrestrial reptiles, they cared for their young. The swathe they had grazed through the woods ran plain to see from the south. Doubtless Bill Svoboda had identified and followed it just as Eva had been doing.

A hill lifted out of the meadowland. On its grassy lower slope the other vehicle had landed, in order to observe the herd at a respectful distance. Not that terasaur were quick to attack. Except for bulls in rut, they had no need to be aggressive. But neither had they reason to be careful of pygmies who stood in their way.

"What's happening?" Eva breathed. "They never act like this—in summer, anyhow."

"They're doing it, though." Dan's words were as jerky as hers.

The car from Anchor was not totally beyond recognition. Tough alloys and synthetics went into any machine built for Rustum. But nothing in the crumpled, smashed, shattered, and scattered ruin was worth salvage. Fuel still oozed from one tank not altogether beaten apart. The liquid added darkness to a ground that huge feet had trampled into mud. Now and then a beast would cross that slipperiness, fall, rise besmeared and roaring to fling itself still more violently into the chaos.

The hillcrest around which the herd ramped was naked stone, thrusting several meters up like a gray cockscomb. There the three humans had scrambled for refuge. The berserk animals couldn't follow them, though often a bull would try, thunder-bawling as he flung himself at the steeps, craned his great wattled neck and snapped his jaws loud enough for Dan to hear through all the distance and tumult. Otherwise the terasaur milled about, bellowed, fought each other with tushes, forelegs, battering tails, lurched away exhausted and bleeding till strength came back to seek a fresh enemy. Several lay dead, or dying with dreadful red slowness, in clouds of carrion bugs.

Females seemed less crazed. They hung about on the fringes of the rioting giants and from time to time galloped clamoring in circles. Terrified and forgotten, the calves huddled by the pool.

High overhead, light seeping through clouds burnished the wings of two spearfowl that waited for their own chance to feast.

"I'd guess—well, this has got to be the way it was," Dan said. "Bill set down where you see. The herd, or some individual members, wandered close. That seemed interesting, no cause for alarm. Probably all three were well away from the car, looking for a good camera angle. Then suddenly came the charge. It was a complete surprise; and you know what speed a terasaur can put on when it wants. They had no time to reach the car and get airborne. They were lucky to make it up onto the rock, where they've been trapped ever since."

"How are they, do you think?" Eva asked.

"Alive, at least. What a nightmare, clinging to those little handholds in darkness, hearing the roars and screams, feeling the rock shiver underneath them! And no air helmets. I wonder why that."

"I daresay they figured they could dispense with apparatus for the short time they planned to be here."

"Still, they've had the nuisance of cycling through pressure change." Dan spoke absently, nearly his whole attention on the scene that filled the lenses. At the back of his mind flickered the thought that, if this had gone for as many hours as evidently was the case, the herd would have wiped itself out by now had it not been handicapped by darkness.

"Well," Eva was saying, "Ralph told me more than once how he longed to really experience the lowlands, if only for a few breaths." Her fist struck the control panel, a soft repeated thud. "Oh, God, the barrier between us!"

"Yes, Mary remarked the same to me. Except I always had too much else to show her and try to make her see the beauty of——"

Bill Svoboda was on his feet, waving. The glasses were powerful; Dan saw how haggard, grimed, and unkempt the man was. Mary looked better. But then, he thought, she would forever. She must in fact be worse off, that bright head whirling and ready to split with pain, that breast a kettle of fire . . . together with hunger, thirst, weariness, terror. She kept seated on her perch, sometimes feebly waving an arm. Her brother stayed sprawled.

"Ralph's the sickest, seems like," Dan went on. "He must be the one most liable to pressure intoxication."

"Let me see!" Eva ripped the binoculars from him.

"Ouch," he said. "Can I have my fingers back, please?"

"This is no time for jokes, Dan Coffin."

"No. I guess not. Although——" He gusted a sigh. "They are alive. No permanent harm done, I'm sure." Relief went through him in such a wave of weakness that he must sit down.

"There will be, if we don't get them to a proper atmosphere in

. . . how long? A few hours?'' Eva lowered the binoculars. ''Well, doubtless a vehicle can arrive from High America before then, if we radio and somebody there acts promptly.''

Dan glanced up at her. Sweat glistened on her face, she breathed hard, and he had rarely seen her this pale. But her jaw was firm and she spoke on a rising note of joy.

''Huh?'' he said. ''What kind of vehicle would that be?''

''We'd better take a minute to think about it.'' She jackknifed herself into the chair beside his. Her smile was bleak. ''Ironic, hm? This colony's had no problems of war or crime—and now, what I'd give for a fighter jet!''

''I don't understand——No, wait. You mean to kill the terasaur?''

''What else? A laser cannon fired from above . . . Aw, no use daydreaming about military apparatus that doesn't exist on Rustum. What do you think about dropping a lot of fulgurite sticks? Bill's dad can supply them from his iron mine.'' She grimaced and lifted a hand. ''I know. A cruel method of slaughter. Most of the beasts'll be disabled only. Well, though, suppose, as soon as our friends have been taken off, suppose a couple of agile men go afoot and put the creatures out of their misery with some such tool as a shaped-charge drill gun.''

Shocked, he exclaimed: ''You'd destroy the entire herd?''

''I'm afraid we must,'' she sighed, ''After all, it's gone crazy.''

''*Why* has it? We've got to find that out, Eva. Otherwise somebody else'll get caught by the same thing, and might not survive.''

She nodded.

''I doubt if we can learn the cause from a lot of mangled dead meat,'' he told her.

''We can arrange experiments on other herds, later.''

''To what effect? Look at the damage here. We could wipe out the terasaur in this entire region. They aren't common; nothing so big can be. But it appears they're mighty damn important to ecology. Have you seen Joe de Smet's paper on how they control firebrush? That's a single item. It'd be strange if there aren't more that we haven't discovered yet.'' Dan gulped. "Besides, they're, oh, wonderful," he said through the tumult below. "I've seen them pass by in dawn mists, more silent than sunrise . . . "

Eva regarded him unbelievingly, until she whispered: "Are you serious? Would you risk Mary Lochaber's life, and two more, to save a few animals?"

"Oh, no. Of course not."

"Then what do you propose?"

"Isn't it obvious? We carry field gear, including a winch and plenty of rope. Lower a line, make them fast, and we'll crank them right up into this car."

She sat for an instant, examining his idea with a fair-mindedness he well knew, before the red head shook. "No," she said. "We can't hover close, or our jet turbulence may knock them right off that precarious perch. Then we'd have to drop the line from our present altitude. This is a windy day; the hill's causing updrafts. I don't expect the end of a rope could come anywhere near—unless we weight it. But then we've made a pendulum for the wind to toss around, and very possibly brain someone or knock him loose. See what tiny slanty spaces they've got to cling to, and think how weakened they are by now."

"Right," he answered, "except for one factor. That weight isn't going to be any unmanageable lump. It's going to be me."

She nearly screamed. One hand flew to her opened mouth. "Dan, no! *Please!*"

Lowland air need not move fast to have a mighty thrust. And the topography here made for more flaws, gusts, and whirlings than was common. To control the winch, Eva had to leave the car on autopilot, which meant it lurched about worse than when hovering under her skilled hands. Dan swung, spun, was yanked savagely up and let drop again, scythed through dizzy arcs, like the clapper of a bell tolled by a lunatic.

The winds thundered and shrilled. Through his skull beat the brawl of jets aimed to slant past him, groundward. Below him the terasaur bellowed and trampled a drumfire out of the earth. Knotted around his waist, the line wouldn't let him fall, but with every motion it dug bruisingly into his belly muscles. He grasped it above his head, to exert some control, and the shivers along it tore at his palms and thrummed in his shoulders. An animal rankness boiled up from the herd, into his nostrils and lungs. He didn't know if that or the gyring made him giddy.

Here came the rock!

Two meters above, he swept through a quarter circle. "Lower away!" he cried futilely. His partner understood, however, and let out some extra rope. His boots reached for solidity. All at once the car stumbled in an air pocket. He fell, snapped to a halt, and saw the cliff face rush toward him. He was about to be dashed against it.

He heaved himself around the cord till he stretched horizontally outward. The curve of his passage whistled him centimeters above bone-shattering impact. He caught a glimpse of Bill Svoboda, wildly staring, and folded his legs in bare time to keep from striking the man.

Then he was past, and swarming up the rope. On the return arc, the soles of his boots made contact with the stone. He let them brake him by friction. It rattled his teeth, but it practically stopped his swinging. The next touch, on the next sway of the pendulum bob—which was himself—came slow and easy. He got his footing and stood among his friends.

Immediately Eva released more rope. Hanging loosely now, it couldn't haul him back if the car should suddenly rise. He sank to the rock and spent a minute sweating, panting, and shuddering.

He noticed Bill crouched at his side. "Are you all right?" the other man babbled. "Lord, what a thing! You might've been killed! Why'd you do it? We could've held out till——"

"You're okay?" Dan croaked.

"Y-yes. That is, the Lochabers are sick, but they ought to recover fast."

Dan crawled on hands and knees to Mary. "I came for you," he said, and held her close. Dazed, she responded only with a mumble. He let her go, rose, and conferred with Bill.

Taking in still more line, they secured bights around bodies at five-meter intervals. Bill would go first, he being in condition to help Eva; next came Ralph; then Mary (as he made her fast, Dan thought what an odd and deep intimacy this was); finally Dan himself, who could best endure the maximum oscillation.

The remnant of the task proved simple. Eva raised the car, at the lowest possible rate, until one by one the four on the rope dangled free in the sky. She continued to rise till they were in calm air. Thereafter she left the vehicle again at hover and winched them in.

Though reduction helmets were always on hand, she depressurized the cabin on the way back to Moondance. The Lochabers sat half asleep, half in a faint. Eva called the station medic. He said the highlanders should stay in the guesthouse till they had regained enough strength for a flight home; but on the basis of Bill's account, he didn't think that would take long, nor that treatment need consist of more than bed rest and nourishment.

Dan spoke little. He was sunk in thought. Directly after landing, he prepared to take off again.

When he had cycled through the lock, he found Eva on hand. The quarters were a dormitory with kitchenette and mini-bath—cramped, austere, and relieved only by windows that gave on a view of lake and forest, but they could never be opened to the breeze that sang outside. Eva had drawn a chair into the narrow aisle between rows of bunks. Ralph lay at her left, Mary at her right. The siblings were in pajamas, propped up on pillows. Nearby stood a vase of triskele that the visitor must have brought. The room had grown vivid with the goldenness of the blossoms, pungent with their summery odor.

Dan halted. Eva had been crying! She'd washed her face afterward, but even though she seldom wept, he knew the traces of it upon her.

"Why hello, stranger," Ralph greeted. His tone was a little mechanical. Both the Lochabers already seemed well on their way back to health—and less than happy. "How did your expedition go?"

"Successful, I think." Dan's gaze went to Mary and would not let itself be hauled away. Her hair was molten amber across the pillows and her eyes like the heavens about High America.

She smiled at him; but the smile was uncertain, even timid.

"How are you doing?" he said, 99 percent to her.

"We're coming along fine." She spoke so low that he had to strain to hear her in this thin air. "Thanks to you."

"Oh, that wasn't much." Curiously, he didn't blush. Rather, he felt the ghost of a chill.

"It was plenty." Ralph's words came firm. He, too, was a leader. "Damn few men could have done what you did, or would have dared to risk their necks like that."

"I did try to talk him out of it," Eva said in a dulled voice.

"A heroic action," Ralph went on. "You saved us several extra hours of suffering. Please don't think we're ungrateful. Still, we can't help wondering. Why?"

"Your lives," Dan answered. "Or, maybe worse, brain damage."

Mary shook her head. "That wasn't at stake, dear, once you'd located us," she said gently. "We could have waited awhile more."

"I couldn't be sure of that," he said, with a slight upstirring of anger that she should be thus withdrawn. "I didn't know how long you'd been marooned, and you just might have been among those people whose pressure tolerance is abnormally low." *As low as mine is high.*

"We aren't," Ralph said. "But anyway, it was quite an exploit, and we owe you our sincerest thanks." He paused. "And then you flew back at once, not even stopping to rest. I stand in awe." He chuckled, though his heart wasn't in it. "Or, I will stand in awe as soon as the doctor lets me out of bed."

Dan was glad to shift the subject. "My job, after all." He drew up a chair to face Eva and them. It was good to sit. Hour upon hour had drained him. (The flight from here to the valley again, through air that in places had gotten heavily turbulent; the hovering above the rampage; the squinting and studying, while the agony of the herd tore in him almost as if it had been his own; the final thing he did; and not even his triumph able to lift the weariness off his bones, during the long flight back.) Maybe he should have caught some sleep after his return, before coming here.

"Was it the terasaur you were concerned about?" Mary

asked. "Eva told us you were going back to them, but she didn't know more than that herself."

He nodded. "Uh-huh. They're an important part of the environment. I couldn't pass up this chance to learn more about them, and try to save what was left."

Eva half rose. Something of the woe behind her eyes disappeared. "Did you?" she cried.

"I think so." A measure of joy woke likewise in him. "Frankly, I feel more like bragging about that than about a bit of athletics at a rope's end."

"What happened? What'd you do?" Eva reached toward him.

He grinned. The tide of his pleasure continued to flow. "Well, you see, terasaur do go rather wild in rutting season. The cause must be a change in body chemistry, whether hormonal or pheromonal we don't know—but we do know how micro amounts of such substances will affect animal behavior, humans included. Now, this herd wasn't mating and its antics were crazy even for that time of year. However, there were certain basic similarities. I wondered what new factor might have triggered the madness."

He stopped for breath. "Go on!" Eva urged.

Dan sought Ralph's gaze. "Petroleum is complicated stuff," he said. "Besides long-chain hydrocarbons, it contains all sorts of aromatics and the chemists alone know what else. In addition, your jet fuel probably has polymers or whatever, produced in the course of refining. My idea was that in among those molecules is one, or a set, that happens to resemble the terasaurian sex agent." Mary drew a gasp. "Not your fault," Dan added hastily. "Nobody could have known. But it does underline the necessity of learning everything we can about this planet, doesn't it?"

The blond young man scowled, "You mean . . . wait a minute," he said. "A few bulls drifted near our car, probably just curious. They got a whiff of unburned fuel dissipating in the exhaust; we'd left the motor idling as a precaution—what we thought was a precaution. That whiff was enough to make them charge, cutting us off from the car. Then, when the first tank was ruptured and fuel spilled out by the hundreds of liters, it drove the entire herd into a frenzy. Is that what you mean?"

Dan nodded again. "Correct. Though of course the total situation was wrong, unbalanced, for the poor beasts. The molecules involved must have similarities but no doubt aren't identical with their natural gonad stimulator. Besides, it's the wrong time of year and so forth. No wonder they ran amok. Suppose someone injected you with an overdose of any important hormone!"

"It's an interesting guess. Are you certain, though?"

"The biochemists will have to check out the details. But, yes, I am certain in a general way. You see, I flitted back to the site, where they were still rampaging. I ignited the spilled fuel with a thermite bomb. It went up fast, in this atmosphere. Almost immediately, the herd started to calm down. By the time I left, the survivors had returned to their calves."

"M-m-m——"

"I know why you're glum, Ralph. Your family business is getting set to produce oil-fired motors. And now it'll have to do a lot of research first. What's at stake isn't merely the terasaur, you realize. It's every related species, maybe the entire lowland ecology."

"That's why you were so anxious to save the herd," Mary said low. "Eva's told us how you insisted."

"Oh, I didn't have any definite ideas at that time," Dan replied. "Only a—a general principle." His mood drooped. Trying to lift it, he said, "This doesn't mean your father's project has to be cancelled. Once the chemicals have been identified, I'm sure they can be taken out of the fuel."

"Indeed." Ralph forced a smile. "You've done us a considerable favor, actually. Besides the rescue, you've saved us a number of further losses like this."

"But you didn't know!" tore from Mary.

Dan started half out of his seat. "What's that?"

"You didn't know—then—and anyway, even if you had known, there are other herds——" She began to weep.

Appalled, he went to her, knelt by her bunk, and gripped her hand. It lay cold and moveless in his. "Mary, what's wrong?"

"I was afraid of this . . . what Ralph and Eva were getting at . . . before you came . . . don't you see? You, you, you care so greatly about this land . . . that to save a part of it . . . you'd risk——"

"Not your life, ever!" he exclaimed.

"No, I s-s-suppose not . . . but your own!"

"Why shouldn't I, if I want to?" he asked in his bewilderment.

Her look was desperate upon him. "I thought—I hoped—All the years we might have had! You risked those!"

"But . . . but Mary, my duty—"

In long, shuddering breaths, she mastered herself enough to say, with even the ghost of a smile: " 'I could not love thee (Dear) so much, Lov'd I not honour more.' Dan, I never really sympathized with that attitude. Or, at least, I think two people have to share the same, well, the same honor, if they really want to, to share each other. We belong to different countries, you and I. Can you understand?"

He shook his head as he spoke, harshly. "No. I'm afraid I don't." He rose to go. "But you're still exhausted, Mary. I'd better not keep after you about this, or anything. Let's talk later, shall we?"

He stooped above her bed, and their lips touched, carefully, as if they were strangers.

Though the air outside was hot and damp, a rising wind roared in treetops; and over the lake came striding the blue-black wall of a rainstorm that would cleanse and cool.

Nobody else was in sight when Dan and Eva left the guesthouse. Nonetheless they did not continue on among the neighbor buildings, but went down to the shore. The water chopped at their feet. Afar, lightning flashes were reflected off its steeliness, and thunder rolled around heaven.

"Well," he said at last, into the wind, "I guess that's that."

"You'll get over it," said Eva, no louder or livelier than he. "You both will, and be friends when you happen to meet."

"Except why couldn't she *see*——?"

"She could, Dan. That's precisely the trouble, or the salvation. She sees far too clearly."

"You mean, because I care about the land, she doesn't imagine I care about her? No! She's not that petty."

"I didn't say she is, Dan. In fact, she's very large, very wise and kind. Look, she *can* live here, never going outside of cages like a house and a helmet. But to make you stay all your days, or more than a bare fragment of them, where she can be—that'd cage you. You, who now have the whole world before you. Better to say goodbye at once, while you're still fond of each other."

And you, Eva, inherit me, he thought in bitterness. He glanced down at her, but her head was averted from him and he saw only flying cinnabar locks.

Wind skirled, thunder cannonaded. He barely heard, after a minute: "That's what I had to tell Ralph before you arrived. When he asked me to marry him."

The breath went from Dan. The first stinging drops of rain smote him in the face.

Then she turned back and took both his hands. In her eyes he saw—not a plea, not an invitation—the challenge to make a new beginning.

Chad Oliver

CARAVANS UNLIMITED: STABILITY

THE great lightship of Caravans, Unlimited came out of the gray wastes of not-space with a shuddering wrench. The ship steadied, at home again in the black velvet of the universe in which it had been born. The symbol on its bow, a laden camel, seemed to breathe a sigh of relief. The system of Capella was almost dangerously close; the tremendous yellow primary, sixteen times the size of the sun that earth knew, blazed against the faint light of more distant stars.

Tucker Olton released himself from his chair clamps and managed a sickly smile. He had never gotten used to the dizzy sensation of returning to normal space. He tried to cover up his discomfort by firing questions at his companion.

"I don't get it," he said. "Your schemes usually make at least a crazy kind of sense to me, but not this time. Exactly what in the hell do you think you're *doing*?"

Alex Porvenir salvaged what he could of his spilled drink and added enough Scotch to make it respectable. "I think it best if I spare you the arcane details on this one. Just do what I tell you and then you can always plead ignorance when everything blows up in my face."

"Don't be avuncular, Alex. It's my responsibility, too, and my job. I have a right to know what's going on."

Alex looked at the younger man, his brown eyes narrowed.

He ran a lean, strong hand through his graying hair. "Don't you trust me, Tuck?"

"Of course, I trust you. That's not the point. *You* aren't trusting *me* and I don't understand why. Your plan won't work and you know it. So what's the deal?"

"Think the old man is losing his grip, do you?"

"I didn't say that. I don't think that. Dammit, we've known each other for a long time. We've worked on a lot of projects together. We've had our disagreements, but I've *never* seen an operation like this one. It's—well, it's just plain silly. You must have your reasons. I merely want to know what they are."

Alex put down his drink and fired up an exceptionally foul pipe. "I have my reasons, yes. I told you why I wanted to leave you out of the planning stage, and I wasn't kidding. My intention is to violate a sacred company directive—I'm disobeying orders, if you want to put it that way. If my plan doesn't work, that's my hard luck. If you weren't involved in it, you're in the clear. Still want to know everything?"

"I want to know *something*."

"Okay. Just to set your feverish brain to rest. I'm very concerned about the Maburu; I've always admired them a great deal. I know their life has been tough, but if I could have picked the person I wanted to be I just might have *been* one of the Maburu. The atavistic streak in me, I suppose—I happen to like hunters."

"But that's exactly what the company wants you to do. We're trying to *preserve* the Maburu culture. . . ."

"Are we?" Alex blew out a cloud of acrid blue smoke. "Maybe it all depends on how we define our terms. I'm worried about what always worries me in these situations—this habit we have of posing as Omnipotent Beings, messing around with other people's lives. Caravans has made mistakes before, and so have we as individuals. We don't know everything. It's all too easy to allow our own interests to shade the decisions we make. Caravans wants those horns; they've been a profitable product for us. When you cut through the high-sounding verbiage about saving the integrity of the Maburu lifeway, what they really want me to do is to see to it that those horns keep coming. I'm not convinced. Maybe that's the best way to proceed, maybe not. I promise you that what I want to try is not unethical. It will violate no laws. Beyond that, I think it'll work—that is, it will attain the basic objectives of the Caravans planners. I'm just not going to do precisely what I was told to do. Let me ask you a question. Will my plan result in any possible harm to the Maburu?''

"I don't know what your plan really is."

"So I'll rephrase my question. You *do* know what action I am going to take. That's what you've been moaning and groaning about. Will it hurt them in any way?"

"No. I don't see——"

"Then can't we leave it at that? Do me a favor this once and don't press me for details. You'll know soon enough."

Tucker Olton sighed. "Okay, Alex. I just hope you know what you're doing."

Alex Porvenir smiled and drained his drink. "So do I, friend. So do I."

The great yellow sun was low in the western sky, burning redly through banks of rain-swollen clouds. Some of the fierce heat had gone out of the day. The winds were beginning, gently now, and they carried a hint of cooling moisture. The plains grasses stirred. Even the thorny flat-topped trees swayed a little, showing signs of life after the searing afternoon heat.

A small herd of about twenty bokix became active in a clump of thick brush. The animals ventured out of the shade for the first time in many hours. They milled about aimlessly, shaking off the torpor of the hot afternoon, sampling the scorched but sweet-smelling grasses.

A large buck lifted his horn-crowned head to taste the wind. He was a splendid creature, his coat delicately striped with tan and white, his liquid eyes clear, his exquisite horns golden and sweeping back over his powerful shoulders. The antelopelike bokix, somewhat resembling the kudu or oryx of ancient earth, were all big animals but the buck was truly exceptional. He must have weighed close to five hundred pounds.

The buck tossed his horns and snorted. He was thirsty after

the heat of the afternoon. He wasted no time on the grass. He moved off with a long, easy stride, headed for water.

The other bokix followed his lead. The herd strung out almost in single file, walking steadily into the wind.

Old, old laws, as old as complex life on the land. Where there are grassy plains, there will be animals that feed on the grasses. Where there are grass-eaters, there will be hunters to prey upon the herds. Lithe, fast killers with sharp claws and teeth. Scavenger packs to snarl over the carcasses. Birds to peck and rip and scratch at the meat-shredded bones.

And, sometimes, men. A special kind of men. Tireless, strong, patient men, their eyes narrowed against the sun and wind. Men who wait and stalk and wait again. Men who know about arrows and poisons and traps. Men who know the land and the animals that live upon the land. Men who know that animals must drink after the heat of the day. Men who know where the springs bubble and the rivers flow. . . .

Hunters.

Waiting.

These, then, are the Maburu.

Hard men; there are no fat Maburu. The men leave their crude brush shelters and seek the herds. The hunting bands are small, six or seven men moving like shadows along dusty and almost invisible trails. The men know their jobs, but foot hunting is slow. Often, they are gone for many days before they make a big-enough kill to justify returning to camp.

The women and the few old men stay fairly close to the shelters. The women fan out, carrying their babies in cape slings, searching for edible roots and berries and the wild succulent melons that grow along the ground vines. They actually supply most of the food; the Maburu could not live on meat alone in their tough world. The women pick up firewood along the way, and when they return to the shelters they build little fires and sit and wait and stare into the gathering darkness. . . .

The older children—there are not many in any one of the scattered Maburu groups—play the games they have always played. The boys build snares and go after lizards and snakes and small rodents with their scaled-down bows and arrows. The girls help with the babies and dig roots out of the hard-packed ground and weave little baskets for berries.

It is not an easy life. There is seldom enough food for a full belly. There are few luxuries. There is sickness that strikes suddenly. There are children who whimper and die, and there are men who do not return. . . .

But there is more than this.

There are times when the big kill is made and there is meat for everone. It has a good smell with the juices dripping into the fires. You can eat until you hurt, and rest, and eat again. You can sleep a long sleep and dream your dreams and be secure in the knowledge that there will be more food tomorrow. There are times for dancing, times for singing happy songs. There are times for jokes, and times when a man and a woman can lie together in the warm huts with the rains drumming on the thatch. There are times when the sky traders come, taking away the golden horns of the bokix and leaving in return wonderful things that give days of enchantment. There are times when a boy comes of age, and you can see pride in his eyes, and it is good to be a Maburu. There are time when a child is born, and you know that the Maburu will go on forever.

Now, while the small band of Maburu hunters deploys in the afternoon sun, dividing along the stream bank and leaving an open corridor so that the bokix will not catch their scent, there are other Maburu.

That is the problem.

They are not far away, these new Maburu. A hard journey of two days, that is all. Looked at in another way, though, the new Maburu are distant indeed.

They are different, and have become more different within the span of two generations.

There are many, while the old Maburu were few. They live close together. Their houses are solidly made, and they do not move them with the seasons.

The men no longer hunt. They spend the long afternoons in councils around great calabashes of sugar-stalk beer. It is a party of sorts, but there is work to be done and they take it seriously.

The councils are forums. There are many legal cases to be heard
and decided. Boundary disputes, and thefts, and endless details
of bridewealth payments.

And witchcraft. There are too many witches. . . .

The doctors are busy indeed. It is difficult to combat the
witches. The doctors must examine the victims. They know that
illness is caused by witches, of course, but that is not specific
enough. They must speak with the spirits, calling to them on
their ornately carved bows with the special strings and the
sounding gourds that resonate when struck. And they must
consult the flashing Wiloto, which can signal answers that only
they can read. Then they know the witch that is responsible, and
what she has done. That is the diagnosis. The treatments are
complicated and expensive, and sometimes they fail. Then the
witch must be confronted directly, and that is a dangerous
business.

The women, too, are busy. They work hard, harder than in
the old way. There is clearing and the planting and the weeding
and the harvesting in a never-ending cycle. There are the great
baskets to weave, some of them as tall as the woman herself; the
baskets have intricate designs of many colors and they are used
to store the foods in stilted storage huts where the rodents cannot
get at them. There is more than one wife in a house now, and that
means trouble. It is small wonder that some of the women turn to
witchcraft and use their ancient power. It gives release of a sort.

The new Maburu have discovered agriculture. They do not
know how remarkable this is. They know only that they can
grow more food than they could ever find. They know only that
it is easier to grow food than to hunt it—easier for the men, at
any rate. They know only that now there is enough food so that
people never have to go to sleep with empty bellies.

They know only that there are more Maburu, and they are not
fools by any means. They know that there is strength in
numbers. They can stay all their lives in one village instead of
wandering the hard trails lean and hungry and shifting camps
with the changing seasons. Their children have a better chance
to survive; no longer must they fear becoming too attached to a
baby that may be dead in a matter of days. Elders are not a rarity

now and a man does not routinely face death when he is thirty.

They rather look down on their backward cousins, these new Maburu. They know that they have found a better way.

Who, after all, would spend his life tired and thirsty on the hunt, when he could sit back in the shade and sip his beer and relish the importance of savoring a good legal case?

Surely they are ignorant, those old Maburu. . . .

The buck paused and lifted his head, his golden horns gleaming in the last rays of the setting sun. He sniffed the freshening wind. There was a faint scent that disturbed him. He hesitated, his white-flecked tail cocked with awareness.

It was the sweet wet smell of water that decided him. He moved again toward the stream.

The bokix herd was not walking now. The gait had shifted to a fast purposeful trot. Dust puffed up around them and behind them.

The buck reached the river first. He waded out in the cool clean water, enjoying the sensation of it. He paused again and froze for a moment, his nostrils quivering. Then he drank, and the herd drank with him.

The Maburu hunters struck. Swiftly, suddenly, soundlessly. Converging, three from upstream and three from down. The first arrows flew while the bokix were still in the water. The animals could not maneuver. They were easy targets.

When the shafts hit, the stricken bokix did not simply roll over in the water and die. They were big animals, and it took a lucky arrow to drop a bokix in his tracks. The herd exploded, thrashing and snorting. There was whirling confusion, with golden horns flashing and red blood mixing with the muddied water.

Most of the animals charged for the bank they had just left, heedless now of the hunters who waited for them. They heaved themselves out of the water and took off at a dead run for the cover of the brushy thickets. They ignored the arrows that pricked at their hides.

The great buck was unhit. Part of the reason was that the hunters were primarily after meat, and the cows were better eating. But the hunters had seen his fantastic horns, and more than one arrow had come his way. It was more than luck. The animal had not attained his size and age without wisdom and cunning. He had survived in a tough world. Even before the arrows had flown, some instinct had warned him. He began to swim away, making for the opposite bank. He was out of effective range before most of the rest of the herd had fully reacted.

The hunters were jubilant. The stalk had been perfect, the arrows true. At least seven of the bokix had been severely pierced. It was an incredible number.

But the hard part was just beginning.

The poison would work, yes; it was fresh and strong and smeared thickly on the foreshafts of the arrows. But the poison worked slowly on large animals. It had to get into the bloodstream, and an animal as big as a bokix would take time to die.

And the bokix would not conveniently stay together, trot back to camp, and collapse. They would split up, go in all directions.

They must be followed along unpredictable trails. They must be found when they weakened, found and guarded. There were other animals who would welcome the Maburu kill, either to bring down the dazed bokix or to scavenge the dead meat. The bokix must be butchered and the flesh cut into long strips to dry; otherwise, the meat was too heavy to carry. Someone had to notify the camp so that the women and children could shoulder some of the burden.

And night was falling. It was no simple matter to track a wounded animal through the darkness.

Still, it had been a great hunt.

It would be good to sit around the fires and tell about it, when and if they got home.

One day, it would be good to remember.

The Caravans lightship drifted in silent orbit, far above the world of Capella VII. It was a creature of the deep, and docked on the shores of that strange space-sea only under the most exceptional circumstances.

The spherical landing shuttles came down out of space, whispering through the atmosphere. There were six of them, floating down like white bubbles through the glare of the warm sunshine.

Many times the traders had come thus to the Maburu, seeking the golden horns of the bokix. The horns were fabulous, natural works of art, but what made them valuable enough to transport was the elementary fact that wild animals were extinct on the human ant hill that was earth. The horns of the bokix were priceless exactly because there was nothing like them at home. The value of a status symbol varies inversely with the supply.

There was no need for the traders to conceal their movements. They had nothing to fear from the Maburu, and indeed they *wanted* to be seen.

But this time they had not come to trade.

This time their task was different. . . .

Emerging from the landing shuttles, the traders greeted the shouting Maburu cordially. There was real friendliness on both sides; they welcomed each other. It was a profitable relationship for both of them, of course, but it was more than that. The traders generally liked and admired the Maburu, and the Maburu had received only good things from the traders. You tend to like people who bring you fine presents.

The traders dealt only with the hunting Maburu. The farmers had no horns.

It takes time to trade, whether you are dealing with primitive or civilized peoples. You don't just dump out your goodies, collect your horns, and leave. That is an insult. No, there must be feasting and songs and pleasant conversation that only lightly touches upon the purpose of the visit. . . .

Days went by before the shuttles were loaded, and still the traders were not through. Trade was not the primary purpose of this visit to the Maburu, although they could not afford to ignore the opportunity to obtain more of the golden horns. The logistics of space travel made it necessary to transact business whenever it was possible. Time spent in space was dead time; it cut into profits.

The traders did not understand the rest of their job at all. Alex Porvenir had asked them to do many peculiar things in his time, but nothing like this. Still, the man knew his job—and his word was law in field operations.

They could not explain to the Maburu. They knew nothing to explain. They just did what they had been told to do.

The traders grumpily shouldered axes and proceeded to a nearby forest. While the Maburu watched and wondered, they selected tall trees and began to chop them down. When they got one down, they trimmed off the branches and converted the trees into long poles. The poles varied in length between fifteen and twenty feet. They were so heavy that it took ten men to haul them from one place to another.

The Maburu thought it was great fun. Besides, there would be firewood for many months.

The traders were much less amused. They could have done the job quickly with the proper energy equipment, of course, but Alex Porvenir had specified axes, picks, and shovels. No doubt it had something to do with the laws governing the introduction of sophisticated technology into undeveloped areas. Just the same, *he* wasn't doing any chopping or hauling.

It seemed to take forever. The men were not in condition for this kind of work. They tired easily in the burning sun. Their hands blistered. Their backs ached.

It took them a solid eight days to cut one hundred poles.

None of them noticed a single landing shuttle that drifted down out of the sky on the fourth day. It did not come down in the usual place. It landed on the edge of one of the new agricultural villages, and one man got out.

If they had noticed, the traders were past caring.

In the manner of men saddled with a difficult and senseless job, they blanked their minds and just tried to get through it. Alex Porvenir would not have won any popularity contests with them. They hated him, they hated Caravans, and before long they hated the Maburu, who finally got bored and left them alone.

When they had cut and trimmed one hundred poles, they dragged and rolled them to the clearing that Porvenir had designated on his map. That took four more days.

Then the real fun began.

The weary and angry men started to dig holes. Deep, deep holes. One hundred of them, arranged in a precise and complicated pattern. The ground was hard and dry and did not yield easily. It was like chipping away at rock.

It did not console them any to remember that the ship could have drilled the holes in a matter of seconds.

The only pleasure they had was in thinking of what all this was costing Caravans. Every hour that ship remained in orbit was lost time. They already *had* the horns.

It took seven days to dig the holes, and they were not pleasant days. The traders muttered sourly about mutiny, and they were only half-joking. But they were too well paid to take the idea seriously. They were also too damned tired.

Besides, they still had to get the poles *into* the holes.

By the time they had rigged up some crude hoists and started to plant the forest of poles in the clearing, they figured they were trapped in some madman's nightmare.

Alex Porvenir's, to be specific.

Poles in the holes. They ran through all the possible variations on that one, most of them obscene.

Mostly, they just wanted it all to be over.

Alex Porvenir stepped out of the shuttle and looked at the village.

He was not unmindful of the crew still chopping down trees in the forest near the camp of the old Maburu. He knew that it was a tough, dirty job. He knew that the skilled men would resent it. Still, it was accomplishing its purpose. His plan was by no means as bizarre as it seemed.

He put the crew out of his mind. His task was here, with the new Maburu. It was all up to him now. If he failed, much more would be lost than a single staple in the interstellar trade. The Maburu themselves were on the line.

Alex smiled. He welcomed the challenge. It was good to get out of the ship, get away from nagging doubts. It was good to feel the land under his feet and the warm sun on his face. It was good to sniff the smells of living things, carried on the wind.

The land and the sky and the sun always restored Alex. Both his mind and his body told him that man was still an animal. He never felt really comfortable sealed in a ship or trapped in the sterile towers of a city. He needed the ancient things.

He was consciously aware of the pleasure he took in functioning as a field anthropologist again, getting ready to do a job he knew he could do well. Scanners and computers were fine and necessary, but sometimes a man had to get out and stick his nose in the dirt. Alex was interested in people. They were lots more fun than elegant abstractions.

He stood in the open, not trying to hide. He lit his pipe, savoring it for a change. He studied the scene before him. He was on a small rise, and his view was clear. He could see a group of Maburu already moving toward him.

The new Maburu. How incredible they were, and how little aware of their own accomplishment!

There was the neat and compact village, with the solid houses and the thick roof thatches yellow-brown in the sun. It was not a small village; Alex estimated that it held at least two thousand people. That meant a population density perhaps fifty times higher than that of the hunting Maburu. There were the fields, radiating out from the village. Not all of them were in production; the ones closest to the village were mostly in fallow, as fresher and more distant land had to be cleared when the original fields played out. The Maburu had no livestock and thus no fertilizer; they did not know how to replenish the soil.

Alex could see, though, that the fields were interplanted. He could recognize four different kinds of plants growing side by side in each sprawling field. That was something.

Capella VII was a big planet, but it was very lightly inhabited. Much of it was water. There were whole continents that were devoid of men. There were other people besides the Maburu, of course, but not many. Man was still a rather rare animal on Capella VII. There was no other agriculture anywhere on the planet.

The Maburu had *invented* it. On earth it had taken man a good two million years to turn the same trick. If it had never happened, Alex would not be where he now was. Crops in the soil provided the roots from which all civilizations grew. Settled villages, states, cities, industry—yes, and space travel itself. It was a monumental accomplishment.

There was another side to the coin. More people meant more problems. Wars and social classes and stinking slums—the Maburu had much to look forward to. But that was a distant future, thousands of years away.

Farming was hell on hunters, too. Hunters need a lot of room, and their small populations cannot compete with organized farmers. There were no hunters left on earth. Ever since the Neolithic, the hunters had dwindled. They had retreated into deserts and arctic wastes, land nobody else wanted. And in time there was nowhere left to go. . . .

The hunting Maburu were already anachronisms, whether they knew it or not. The invention of agriculture had made them obsolete. In the long run, they were doomed. It did not matter how brave they were, or how admirable.

It did matter, perhaps, that Alex happened to like the old Maburu. It did matter that Caravans *needed* the old Maburu.

That was the new factor in the equation: Alex Porvenir and what he knew. He could preserve the old way, with a little luck. Those were his instructions. Those were also his inclinations.

He carefully knocked out his pipe and moved to greet the oncoming Maburu.

It was neither a true first-contact situation nor a simple matter of slipping into an established routine. The village Maburu did not know who Alex Porvenir was, of course, but they did know about the traders from the sky. They were not totally divorced from their hunting kinsmen; they were only separated from them by a journey of two days, and it was by no means unusual for a hunting family to drift over and join the farmers.

It was difficult, as it always was. Difficult and slow. It was complicated by the pressure of time. If Alex's plan was going to work, it had to work quickly. He had to finish his job before those poles were set into the soil.

He had one thing going for him: He could speak the language, after a fashion. He had dealt with the old Maburu many times, and the language of the villagers had not been isolated long enough to change appreciably.

He did not feel that he was in any particular personal danger. The people had no reason to fear him, and he was experienced enough not to make stupid mistakes. On the other hand, he had to be careful. He did not really know these new Maburu. A thickly settled farming village was a far cry from an open hunting band.

A stranger would be studied by many eyes.

There would be whispers and suspicions, and the witches would finger their bones. . . .

Alex smiled and tried to look as inoffensive as possible. He jumped twice in greeting and clasped his hands.

"I come in peace," he said.

The first hours were chaotic, as always. It was impossible for Alex to make any precise observations. It was all a confused blur of smells (greasy wood smoke staining the roof thatch, dry plants splitting in hot granaries, human dung smothered in clouds of flies), colors (faded red cloaks, dirty white feathers, a brilliant blue design on a huge basket, the hard brown of the trampled soil), and sounds (the jabber of too many voices, distant shouts, the creak of wood in the houses, the clacking of bows, the shuffling of naked feet).

He kept smiling, although his head was killing him. He tried to locate a child to make friends with; that was always a good move, but he never had the opportunity. The most he saw of children were round frightened eyes peering out of doorways.

He had hoped that there might be a chief of some sort; it would be easier to deal with a single man. But it rapidly became apparent that there was no chief. These people were acephalous, like so many village farmers. He would probably have to work through a council of elders, and *that* was always a mess.

And slow.

He smiled; he could not afford impatience. He allowed himself to be led. When he was offered food, he accepted. That was often the supreme test for an anthropologist; he had eaten some decidedly grim items in his time. The food given to him wasn't bad, though—a calabash of hot grainy gruel topped with a thick savory sauce.

He asked for water and got it in another calabash. It was very warm and he could almost see the bugs in it. He drank it, anyway, adding a pill on the sly.

When the cooling darkness came, there was the inevitable dancing in a centrally located clearing. It seemed to Alex that this was a maxim among many peoples that he had known: when in doubt how to deal with a stranger, put on a dance.

It gave the visitor something to do.

It also stalled for time. It was the younger people who danced. The elders were free to cluster in groups beyond the firelight, talking and gesturing.

Alex knew that he was being closely observed. He was quite tired, but he kept a fascinated expression on his face. He was actually bored stiff; he had seen it all before, with every imaginable variation. The only aspect that intrigued him was the almost total lack of instrumental background. The Maburu had no drums, no rattles, no string or wind instruments. They simply clicked wooden blocks together to keep time.

The singing was something else again. The Maburu had always been a singing people; they had a flair for poetic imagery, and their mood songs had frequently intrigued the traders who heard them. The hunters sang lonely little songs as they wandered the trails, and their women sang sad laments around their tiny fires. When there was meat from a good kill, there were happy songs.

The songs he now heard were new songs with complex interweavings of rhythms and counter-melodies. They were sung both by the dancers and the audience. Alex recorded as many of them as he could. There might be something useful there.

His attention wandered despite his certain knowledge that he was under close scrutiny.

He was in a hurry, but there was nothing he could do.

In his weariness, he thought:

Again, a man in a village. I have seen so many of them, on so

*many different worlds. I see the correspondences, the parallels.
That is my training. But every village is unique, and every
person.*

There are some things I can anticipate, predict.

*There are other things that will surprise me—perhaps
fatally.*

*I am forever an outsider, always on the fringes. I can try to
understand, but I cannot truly participate. I cannot share.*

*I am alone here, alone in a crowd. I am isolated by what I am
and what I know. I am cut off from all these people, as finally as
the metallic hull of my ship shields me from the abyss of space.*

Again, a man in a village.

The fires eventually died and the dancing stopped.

Alex was escorted to a house not far from the center of the
village. The house was empty now, but the smells and the clutter
testified to the fact that a family had been rather hastily evicted.

He was left alone.

He fumbled around with the aid of his pocket light and located
a pile of moderately clean bedding. He climbed in, fully
dressed, and waited for sleep.

It was a long time coming.

He lay in the darkness, his eyes wide open, listening to the
scrabbling of tiny feet in the roof thatch over his head.

After some hours, he slept.

The first day was over.

There is waste-time, lost-time, in any field investigation. No
matter what pressures you are under, there are certain things that
you must do.

Here, there was seemingly endless discussion with the village
elders who ultimately made whatever decisions were made.
There was the careful cultivation of alliances, the constant
refutation of rumors. There were people to meet, people to
avoid. There were the usual time-consuming mechanics of
housekeeping. Where do you get your food? Who cooks it?
Where does the firewood come from? Who hauls the water?

And always, you must explain and explain and explain.

Alex had no time to spare. As the days went by, he knew that the men from the ship were cutting and trimming the poles, dragging them into position, executing his plan.

He did finally accomplish a few useful things.

He got a basket—

Peering into the stilt-supported granary, he was astonished at the size of the thing. The basket nearly filled the storage room. It must have been lowered into the structure before the roof was finished.

The basket was beautifully made. Tightly and intricately woven, it was covered with a brilliant blue design. The craftsmanship was all the more amazing because the basket was made to be used in everyday life; it was not a ceremonial object. Moreover, it was hidden from view inside the granary.

He gave very close attention to baskets. They were far superior to the relatively crude portable containers of the hunting Maburu.

He found a woman weaving a large basket that was nearly finished. He made a deal with her and arranged to pick the basket up when the design was completed.

That was something.

He recorded songs—

He went with the women into the fields. After they had gotten used to his presence, and had answered his questions about the agricultural cycle, they went on with their work. They sang soft little songs, individual songs, songs that told of drudgery and green living things and the magic of water and the solace of children.

He spent time with boys and girls, recording the songs that went with their games. He sat with the men at beer parties, catching songs that were partly drinking songs and partly long narrative chants that reviewed the surprising details of old legal cases.

The songs were good ones, and he got a lot of them.

And, with excitement, he got the Wiloto—

The old doctor was reluctant at first. He sat cross-legged in his smoky shadowed hut. His bright eyes were studiously blank. He knew nothing. He had no secrets. He was not really a doctor at all. Alex had been misinformed.

Alex persisted. He knew about medicine men. They were

always special, always intelligent, always devious. Where there were witches, there were witch doctors. That was what a witch doctor was—a doctor that treated illness caused by witchcraft. The more serious the witchcraft problem, the more elaborate the techniques of the witch doctors tended to be.

And the new Maburu were infested by witches. It was a characteristic of densely populated farming villages.

So Alex stuck with it. He worked on the old boy, spent long hours with him, gave him presents. He showed him a trick or two that he had learned from other doctors on other worlds. He got his confidence.

And then he got the Wiloto.

The doctor sat impassively in the smoke-filled hut. He had his special bow resting across his knees. He wore a greasy cloak and a kind of square cap made of some faded animal skin.

Alex stayed back in the shadows.

The patient came in. He was a man about thirty years old. He was very thin and his hands were trembling. He could hardly walk. There was a film of sweat on his face. His eyes were clouded and dull.

The man sat before the doctor, swaying. He was close to collapse.

"I am bewitched," he whispered. "I cannot eat. I am in pain. At night, I cannot sleep. You must help me. I will pay you well."

The doctor smiled a toothless smile. "I know you, Kilatya. I know your family. You will be cured."

"The witches——"

"I will know the witches and deal with them. That is why you came to me. It is good that you got here in time. Now, be silent. There are—others—who will help."

The doctor picked up his bow. It was ornately carved and had a very thin, tight gut string. Half of a hollow gourd was inserted between the string and the bowshaft. He held the bow in one hand, the end against his shoulder, like a man playing a violin.

He took a short wand of polished wood and worked it over the taut bowstring, sometimes tapping it and sometimes sawing on it.

The effect was eerie in the gloomy hut.

The doctor began to chant in a monotone, calling on the ancestors. Other voices seemed to answer him, coming from the floor, the roof, the corners of the hut.

Alex smiled. The old boy was some ventriloquist.

The doctor put down his bow. "There, Kilatya. We know the names of the witches. It is as you suspected. There are two of them—your mother's brother's wife and the older sister of your second wife."

Kilatya groaned. "I knew it, I knew it. They will surely kill me."

"No. There are ways. We will consult the Wiloto."

Kilatya trembled violently and was silent.

The doctor reached behind him and picked up a large object wrapped in a red cloth. He placed it between his legs. Slowly, he removed the cloth.

The Wiloto was a squat black pot. It sat on an attached tripod. It was covered with ivory-skull designs. The whole thing was about two feet high.

The doctor put his arms around the Wiloto, embracing it. He began to moan softly. His eyes grew very large and bright.

He put questions to the Wiloto.

The Wiloto answered him. In the gloom of the smoky hut, the Wiloto flashed blue signals. It was like a code of blinking blue light. The strange blue glow illuminated the hunching doctor's face, on and off, on and off. . . .

"There," the doctor said finally. "Now we know what to do." He replaced the Wiloto in its red cloth and set it gingerly aside. He reached out and touched his patient comfortingly. "Follow my instructions, Kilatya, and you will be well again. You need fear the witches no more."

He gave detailed orders about certain herbs, specific prayers, and precise protective spells. Then he sent Kilatya on his way. The man seemed stronger already.

"Very good," Alex said, stepping out of the shadows. "I am impressed with your skill. I am impressed also by the Wiloto. Let me see it again, please."

The old doctor smiled a sly smile and removed the red cloth. "See," he said. "There is a shutter here." He touched the neck of the black pot. "You squeeze it and it opens. Press it again and it closes." He demonstrated.

"And the blue light?"

"There is a large glow-rock inside. It shines in the dark. I know where there are many such stones. It was a simple matter to build the Wiloto. The skill comes in knowing how to use it. A doctor must know many things."

Alex breathed a sigh of relief. He had confidence in this one.

He spent the better part of two days with the doctor, explaining and offering and persuading.

Then he left as he had come, in the landing shuttle.

He carried with him his basket, his songs, and the Wiloto.

He figured that he had two days left before all the poles were in place.

Alex Porvenir felt good. He was very tired, but he was happy. He had been with Helen. He had eaten enough food to last him a week. The computer analysis was favorable.

And he was *clean*.

He fired up his pipe. Even that tasted good.

"Okay, Carlos," he said. "You've seen the analysis. What's your verdict?"

Carlos Coyanosa stared dubiously at the squat black pot with its design of ivory skulls. "Maybe I'm a little dense, Alex. I don't quite get it."

"It's simplicity itself. Allow me to spell it out. The village Maburu make the Wiloto. We can get a good supply once we set up the market in the village. The computer says it will sell. It's a fad item, to be sure, but a durable one. The supernatural is hot right now. There's *nothing* like the Wiloto on earth, and never has been. A for-sure witch doctor's oath pot, complete with skulls and a phosphorescent blue alien stone! Man, Caravans will make a killing on this one. The Wiloto will be so far in, it will stick out the other side!"

Carlos Coyanosa was a cautious man. As the senior Caravans representative aboard the lightship, he *had* to be. "Maybe, Alex. It looks good. I think it will make a profit for us. But exactly how does it tie in with our supply of bokix horns?"

Alex smiled broadly, with rather more confidence than he felt. "Inversely," he said.

"I still don't get it."

"Look at it this way." Alex knew he was on very thin ice. He adopted a very positive tone. "Caravans was getting a good product from the Maburu—bokix horns. The supply of that product was endangered because the Maburu were shifting away from a hunting style of life. My assignment was to maintain the Maburu as a product source. Okay, I've done that. We still have the Maburu, and we've got a product. We've simply exchanged bokix horns for the Wiloto. Everybody wins."

Carlos Coyanosa stared at him. "You *knew* that your instructions meant that you should find a way to keep the bokix horns coming. You're not a fool, Alex. Don't play dumb with me."

"I hope I'm not a fool," Alex carefully refilled his pipe and lit it. "I hope you're not, either. There was only one way I could ensure the supply of bokix horns for the long haul. That way was clearly illegal. It would have involved not only cultural manipulation that was not in the best interests of the people concerned, but also an effort on our part to *retard* normal cultural development. When the ET Council of the U.N. got hold of that one, it would blow us right out of the tub. I just couldn't put Caravans in that position. If we want to go to the top with it, I doubt very much that Caravans will wish to argue that their plan involved suppression of cultural progress in order to preserve a profit. Do I make my point?"

Carlos Coyanosa was not a happy man. He suffered in silence for a very long two minutes. He weighed the alternatives. "You've done a remarkable piece of work," he said finally.

"You do get the point."

"I'd say that you'd made it crystal clear. What in the hell would you have done if there hadn't *been* any Wiloto? I couldn't sell those songs and we couldn't push fifty giant baskets in fifty years."

Alex smiled again. "I guess I'd just have stayed in that village. I always wanted to settle down, put down some roots—and the beer wasn't half bad."

"I hope your dream comes true in the near future," Carlos Coyanosa said sincerely, and left to file his report.

"Look, I *like* hunters." Alex Porvenir relaxed and sipped his Scotch. "Given my druthers, I'd stick with the old Maburu and more power to 'em."

"You sold them right smack down the river," Tucker Olton said.

"How do you figure that?"

"You could have saved them. You didn't even try."

"Saved them from what? And how? The Maburu who still want to hunt can do so; they've got a free choice. We can still market a few bokix horns along with the Wiloto; they are not mutually exclusive. And the farming Maburu are people, too. Don't forget that."

"Those hunters are doomed and you know it."

"In time, yes. In the long run, they can't compete with the farmers for land and resources. But I didn't do that, Tuck. I didn't invent sociocultural natural selection, and I didn't teach those people how to plant crops."

"In fact, you didn't *do* anything."

Alex killed his drink and fixed another. "One thing you still have to learn, my friend. There are times, Caravans or no Caravans, when the best course of action is to do nothing at all. Just leave people alone. There are other times, of course, when you must act. But we play God too easily. It's a disease of power."

"I still don't see——"

"Why I didn't do something to preserve the hunters? I hate to be corny, but it would have been *wrong*. They appeal to me, they appeal to you, but so what? We can't stick them on a reservation or stuff them as exhibits in a museum. What we've really got down there is a selfish situation. It takes a stable culture to guarantee a steady product flow—in this case, bokix horns. When the culture becomes unstable—when it starts to change—it's only natural for Caravans to think in terms of putting the lid on. We want the original product because that's what we're geared to handle. But the Maburu are *evolving* whether they know it or not. This isn't simply a case of some minor deviation that interferes with normal hunting. They have discovered agriculture, just as we did more than ten thousand years ago. The only way to stop them would be to deny them the right to their own future, whatever it turns out to be. We can't force them *backward*—or at least I can't.''

"Just let Mother Nature take her course, eh?"

"Sometimes the old gal knows what she's doing."

"It seems an odd thing for a man with your job to be saying, Alex."

"Sometimes we can help her along a little—for our own interests, or that of Caravans, or to assist people in a really desperate situation. I've never argued that it's *always* wrong to act when you're in the right place at the right time. But, dammit, it's not for us to sit on the sidelines and make romantic judgments about who is to survive and who is to go under. We're not that smart—and we're not that objective, either.''

"And all that jazz about cutting the poles and arranging them in neat little holes? What was *that* all about?"

Alex grinned. "Nothing. Nothing and everything. I had to take some action that would satisfy my superiors. So I took some action—I sent in a crew and put them to work doing something mysterious. The big boys never understand what we're doing, anyway. Cutting the trees and shaping the poles and setting them up—it didn't *hurt* anyone and it bought me the time to find a substitute product. That's all. It was one of my better plans, I think."

"That crew that broke their backs down there for weeks might not look at it that way. I'm glad *I* don't have to face them and give them the word."

"There's no need for them to know, Tuck. We had a plan. They did their part. The plan worked. They weren't wasting their time and effort. Let's leave it at that.''

"Okay." The younger man poured himself a drink. "And after all your work, what have we got?"

"Well, we've got the Wiloto. And we can sleep nights."

"And the Maburu? What have they got?"

Alex Porvenir clasped his hands. "Maybe I'm getting old,

Tuck. But we've given the Maburu the chance to be themselves. We've given them the right to go their own way, wherever it leads. I think that's enough. I'm content, for once.''

The two men looked at each other, thinking of all the decisions they had made in the past and would have to make in the future.

''I'll drink to that,'' Tucker Olton said.

Thomas N. Scortia

THE ARMAGEDDON TAPES
—TAPE II

UNTIL this moment human institutions such as the well-named "Holy State" represented the closest human approach to group consciousness. Yet, there was a deeper racial consciousness that could find expression only in the final melding of two great races, the human and the Angae. These insectlike creatures shared in a unique racial immortality that might never have become part of the total human experience had not the Angae encountered the Children of Men by the merest coincidence. For mankind then, only a focal point, a Messiah was needed and in the outcast Martin, there arose a power and force that spelled the end of the racial uniqueness of the Angae and of humans and eventually the only force that could meet the enveloping destructiveness of the Theos that had now invested the whole of the neighboring *galaxy*. . . .

Die Anelan de Galactea-Vol. II, Ca. 4300

"Second Battalion . . . we are in position now."

"Air assault . . . ETA ten seconds . . . The yellow jump light has been. . . ."

"Mobiles two and three . . . We see them below. The men of the village are gathered in the square. Many of them are in their old ceremonial costumes. They stand, impassive waiting . . . I see the children now. There are six of them. I can identify the

one called Martin through the periscope. He's taller and seems
in command. He is. . . ."

"What are they doing?"

"Attack, attack, attack. . . ."

"Oh, God. . . ."

"It's too much to. . . ."

(Cut the tape. There's nothing beyond this point, only a mass
of confused signals. We're still not sure of what happened in
Cherokee, only that we have lost all contact with our forces and
the mission seems to have failed utterly.)

(How can that be, Inquisitor Jarvis? They were only a handful
and our men are as completely loyal and disciplined as have ever
appeared on the face of the earth.)

(It had happened. Make no mistake of that. These
proceedings are to be considered top secret. You are the only
civilian who knows of this debacle. Naturally, the citizens of
our Holy State must not know. You will forget it when you leave
this room.)

(But there must be an accounting. No citizen may be interrogated or erased without an accounting.)

(Don't be a fool. This is an emergency. All special rights of
the citizen are suspended, especially the rights of these
renegades. Citizen Clawson, you have examined the outcast?)

(John Talltrees? Barbarous name.)

(The Indians love their native names. No matter, the Holy
State has indulged them and preserved their race for reasons
known to it. I suppose its motive as much as anything is to define
their special biochemical immunity to the Mettler serum that has
given us the final world-wide peace for which the human race
has longed.)

(They represent the focal point of a contamination. I would
have eliminated them long ago.)

(You question the decision?)

(No, Inquisitor Jarvis. No, of course not.)

(Then tell me about this John Talltrees. You have had him for
five days. In what fashion has his biochemistry changed? I
gather from your preliminary reports that it has.)

(It's somewhat difficult to define. There are metabolites in the urine, for instance, that are normally associated with paranoid schizophrenia. The acetylcholine esterase of the nervous system has been subtly modified so that the catalytic rate is much enhanced.)

(This means nothing to me.)

(It means that the impulses in his nervous system travel at several times normal speed. His physical reactions are appropriately speeded up as well as his heartbeat and certain parts of his metabolism, most notably his ability to mobilize blood glucose from stored glycogen.)

(And the end result of this is. . . .)

(A remarkably improved human being. He thinks faster, acts faster, and mobilizes greater stress reserves than are available to the normal human being. With all this, he has developed a peculiar psychological dichotomy.)

(Psychological dichotomy?)

(He believes he is two personalities inhabiting a single human body. He does not find this abnormal or alarming or in any way disconcerting. He holds that these will eventually merge and further merge with others. What others, I cannot understand from his interrogation.)

(You've dared to interrogate him without an inquisitor present? You tread on a very dangerous group, Citizen.)

(A purely clinical interrogation, Inquisitor. I recognize that this case is your special interest. I have attempted no deep probe, only what is necessary to elicit a complete case history for your inspection.)

(Very well. This is not for me to decide in any event. Whoever finally disposes of this case will have these tapes for his decision.)

(These tapes?)

(This one and the one with the boy Martin. You are not aware of that one and, unless it seems advisable, you will not be allowed to hear it. I may in due course give you some major information from the tape, however, if it seems useful to your purpose.)

(I want no information of this sort. I'm a citizen, loyal to the State and its avatar, the Premier Annointed. I have every reason to believe he will fill his allotted life span.)

(This is for me to decide, Citizen. Do you question that?)

(State, no.)

(Very well, have your people bring in the subject. We will proceed with the interrogation proper.)

(I will of course leave.)

(Not at all. In such a situation, I will need you as a witness.)

(The tape should be sufficient. Please, the tape should be sufficient. I have no desire. . . .)

(Your desire is to serve the Holy State and at the moment I have the power to decide how the State is served.)

(Very well, I will give the signal.)

(Noise in the background, sound of rolling wheels. Mumbled conversation and the whisper of a door closing.)

(Is he conscious?)

(Yes, Inquisitor.)

(Will you recite the ritual introduction?)

(I would have thought that was a privilege you reserved for yourself.)

(The Holy State looks to all of its citizens as priests of the new scheme.)

(Very well . . . mumble, mumble . . . the Holy Fight of the citizen as a unit of the vast State . . . mumble . . . conceived in the light of the true liberty that is the surrender of self . . . mumble . . . most Exalted Plurality, the Premier Anointed . . .)

(You have no feeling for the words. No matter, there is little doubt that you believe them. Mettler gave us the greatest and most effective tool to assure the continuity of the ecclesiastic reverence in the individual.)

(Shall we begin? Yes? Very well, what is your name?)

My name is John Talltrees and my name is Martin.

(Of course, of course, but which am I addressing?)

For the moment I, John Talltrees, will talk for us. Martin is of the opinion that you cannot fully understand his psychology, which is, after all, alien to your mind. It is a matter of having spent too much time with Them.

(The insect creatures that we destroyed in the spaceship? Was he truly a part of them?)

Body, soul, mind. A complete blending of consciousness, which is why he still holds a deep affection for them even though he now realizes that his species must destroy them or . . . at least absorb them.

(John, what happened in Cherokee? We know that the ship landed or was forced down and that for a long time, the children were among you. We know that the aliens were somehow cast into a kind of trance that was apparently the doing of the children. We know that the children in some fashion entered your society and changed you, but the motives . . . the details, the reasons? . . .)

(Your questions are not phrased precisely enough, Citizen.)

(Your indulgence, Inquisitor, I will pursue this in a fashion that will give us the information we want.)

I am John Talltrees. I have lived in the village of Cherokee in the Great Smokies all of my life, long before you people assembled all the disparate tribes of the land and brought them to our land. I grew up in the gentle hills with their wealth of pine that you have despoiled, the thriving kudzu that would cover whole hills in a summer.

(Kudzu, isn't that a Japanese vine?)

(It is, Inquisitor, introduced in the fifties as a soil stabilizer by the highway builders of the Republican period. It has come to contaminate the area.)

We lived as brothers in the village. Although our numbers had been sadly reduced by the tender angels of the Holy State, there were enough of us to form a viable society and the State for the most part left us alone after it had sequestered us. How were we to know that our sin was one over which we had no control, that we were immune to the nucleic-acid serum that had finally brought peace and conformity to the world, that had brought this antlike dependence upon the State?

(The greatest invention for peace and human dignity, he speaks of it in such a contemptuous manner.)

(Remember, Inquisitor, these are the outcasts. It was for this original sin that they were expelled from our society.)

Oh, like all humans we longed for that special feeling of identity with a larger group. In our case, the identity was the tribe and later the village. We understood your need for it was our need. You, on the other hand, rejected us because we could not fulfill the need in your specific fashion.

(He does not sound like John Talltrees now.)

(It is the other personality intruding.)

(Disgusting.)

When the ship came from the sky, we thought that it was another of your war machines, sent to exterminate us. We knew that you would eventually have to make this particular decision. We were a pocket of infection that could not forever be tolerated. When the ship plunged from the sky and fell onto the mountainside, we ran to the hill spots we had prepared. Many of our people were caught in the valleys and a few were within the area where the ship landed and were never heard from again. It was, we think, the radiation from the ship's engines.

When we finally approached the ship, we found that it was wounded and that there were humans inside. They were children and they came from the ship and greeted us. There were also other things in the ship, great insectlike creatures, but these were either dead or in a deep stupor. The children were very strange . . . filthy and half-blinded by the day's light . . . told us that they had put the aliens to sleep, that some of the aliens had inadvertently been killed. The children stood among themselves and sorrowed over the ones they had killed because they did not want to take life needlessly. They felt all life substance should be conserved for the group and the lost aliens would not be salvaged for the group. One of the children was dead and this one they ate.

(Ugh, Holy Writ, is it true that they were cannibals, Inquisitor?)

(The earlier tape in which the one Martin was interrogated suggested the aliens were. Apparently the children were good students, far too good.)

They explained that this was not a mere ritual, that the aliens had changed them in such a way that they could preserve the essence of each individual by consuming him, that the personality continued as a live thing within the one who had consumed him. It was the most complete kind of personal immortality.

(State, State, can it be? It's what we have always striven for, but can it be?)

(Citizen, you astonish me. This is completely outside of doctrine. Utter political blasphemy. Personal immortality lies only in the continuity of the Holy State.)

(Still, it would make some sense. We know that the personality is an incredibly complex coda, impressed on DNA molecules. If these could be ingested intact and preserved, passed from generation to generation, there would be no true death.)

(It is against all State teachings. Have a care that you don't find yourself in our Chambers of Love.)

(No, no, I don't consider it seriously. I am completely doctrinaire. How could I be otherwise?)

(Of course, Citizen. Of course.)

We took them into our village and tended their wounds and fed them. It was strange. They could not at first eat our food but preferred a sort of reed mash with which we fed our cattle. The one named Martin . . . although it is difficult to decide which of the five children is Martin . . . brought them together and they stood for an hour in silent communion in the square. After that, they could eat our fare. Martin told me that they had changed themselves. In due course, he promised me that they would change us and I found this frightening. I told him that he should not do this but he brushed it aside, saying that they had in the long days and nights of the ship conceived that their existence was not accidental, that they had a special mission for the race from which they sprang.

(This is the crux of the investigation, Citizen. This paranoid delusion of a special mission. Martin spoke of it in the earlier interrogation.)

(Did the interrogator understand what he meant?)

(Alas, he is no longer available for questioning. He had to be sent to the Blessed Fields. He was hopelessly insane.)

(Peace and joy to his soul, Inquisitor.)

(To be sure. John Talltrees, what happened in the village?)

You know what happened initially. Your stations had traced the ship to our village, but for a long time you were content to watch and wait for any overt move. When this did not come, you grew restive and fearful, just as Martin predicted you would. Your fear was too great to be contained and he reached out and stimulated it.

(You imply that he could in some fashion control us?)

The aliens had changed Martin and his companions in many ways, biochemically and physically. What they did not know was that Martin and his companions had been brought by their parents to a remote spot in Canada because they were different, because they would have been exterminated by your Holy State before they could reach maturity, had the State known of them. Because of this special ability of theirs, they were able to identify more closely with the aliens that captured them and their parents than any normal child. They became essentially generators of food for the aliens much as an aphid generates food for ants, and in the process they became a part of the group mind of the aliens. Through that link, they learned to see the universe as the aliens did, to detect the fine structure of physical phenomena in a fashion our gross senses cannot. To detect is to know, to know is to understand, to understand is to manipulate.

(You see, Citizen, it is as we thought. These creatures pose a deadly threat to our Holy State. And to you, John Talltrees. You should have killed them immediately.)

I could not.

(Why not?)

We were friends.

(Friends with filth?)

Friends and a part of them. We took them into our village and Martin and I found that, in spite of his utterly alien way of thinking, that we could somehow communicate on an emotional level. You must understand that, for all of his unusual life and his remarkable talents, he was still little more than a child. Physically about seventeen, he seemed younger and more naive than this in many ways. At first, he even had trouble coordinating his muscles and would often stumble on the road or reach for a glass of water and overshoot it by as much as four inches.

We did not, at the time, recognize the five children for what they were. We saw a startling unity among them, an ability at times almost to merge into a single personality. We found their quiet assurance that they carried some special message for humanity disconcerting. This . . . what Sarah Running Brook called "messianic conviction" . . . was unshakable, a sense of almost holy conviction. Of course, living as outcasts in your Holy State, we were quite familiar with this form of paranoia and made allowances for it.

(Inquisitor, dare we let him go on? To insult the State? Surely, he becomes a candidate for the Fields.)

(Enough of that. The State will dispose of him in due course. For the moment he is valuable to us.)

I took Martin to me as a second son and taught him in those early days to walk and ride and hunt. We hunt a great deal in the old manner of our fathers and he found this strange and primitively satisfying. The two girls became adept at the looms and wove some marvelous fabrics that brought a high return at the State Store. The strangest thing was that, when one of the children developed a talent, suddenly they all seemed to have it. One day, although by our standards it was not seemly, Martin took over a loom from the small one named Beth and produced a fabric with a woof and warp that seemed to interchange, creating a fabric of suppleness and electric quality. He said that he had altered the electrostatic distribution along the cotton molecule, but we passed it off as another of those inexplicable things that children were constantly saying.

You understand, all this while your people were playing a waiting game, fearful of this great ship that had descended into the Smokies. You were completely unaware that the creatures inside were either dead or had been immobilized by the children. That was something I did not understand until much later Martin and I became . . . well . . . closer. They had lived with the aliens for a long time as their food sources . . . Martin called them "cows," which was a reasonably good description for the ant-aphid relationship they had . . . and had developed an empathy for the aliens. Martin always referred to them simply as "They" and he spoke of the love that they had developed for these creatures in the dank confines of the ship. Still, the aliens had denied them their birthright, and as they grew to be more powerful than the aliens, they turned against them. They loved them as children loved their parents and they hated them for the restrictions the aliens placed on their natural talents. When the children finally took over the ship and landed it near our village, they threw the aliens into a deep sleep. Some of them did not survive and died on landing. The children felt a perverse joy in this. They were not truly dead, of course, not so long as members of Their race still lived to eat them.

(God, that reference to cannibalism again, Inquisitor.)

(God? Citizen. You forget yourself. Haven't we of the Holy State spent a good portion of your conditioning demonstrating to you that there is no God, that the State is the sublime summation of all human effort, and that the citizen may lose himself in his fellows? What need do you have for a God?)

(It was a purely automatic response that. . . .)

(Should not have come. Your conditioning leaves something to be desired.)

(No, no, it isn't true. I was one of the first. My parents volunteered for the serum in the midst of the devastating wars when it seemed that the whole race would die.)

(We shall see. When this is finished. . . .)

(I can only await your benign decision, Inquisitor.)

Martin lacked humanity, if you understand me. He knew as did the others that he had a mission. How it came to him I'm not sure . . . probably from what he had seen in the minds of the aliens . . . but he could see clearly into the probable futures of our race and he knew that he had to guide us in a certain direction, that eventually, for our mutual survival before a greater menace we would have to merge with the aliens from whose ship he had come. "They will resist that with all the elemental fury of a total race," he said, "but we will prevail in the end."

I could not understand that since he had assured me that the aliens were not malign, that They sought merely another world, an uninhabited one so that They might again build the culture that had been destroyed in a great disaster in the next Galaxy. They had fled some overwhelming menace that had produced this disaster. A single vast creature, Martin thought.

Yet, although They had no inimical designs on the earth and on our race, Martin knew that They would finally recognize the challenge of the children. He knew that the great ships still waiting beyond the clouds of our world would now not simply go away as They had planned originally. The menace of the children to Their uniqueness as a race and eventually of the human race was too great, the danger to Them too acute. "They will not go," he told me. "They will come finally, reluctantly, and then we will face the Armageddon that will yield a Galaxy-spanning welding of the two races. There will be other races and we will invest the total universe against the day when Something comes."

"Something?" I asked.

Martin shivered. "A menace beyond defining, a thing beyond your wildest imaginings of dread and evil."

I found his wide-eyed horror amusing. He believed in what he said, of course, but I still found it amusing. Why, I don't know since it became obvious that he and the children had an acuteness of vision not given to ordinary human beings.

(Acuteness of vision? In what fashion? You've referred to this before.)

This is a difficult thing for me to understand. As I said, the children had learned from the aliens to see the fine structure of the universe. Where our senses yield a statistical result, a gross summation of minute changes, the children could see on a finer level, determine the subtle interactions of billions of particles, see discretely the tiny forces that made up the larger ones that we detect and deal with. To this end, their senses went beyond the statistical and their manipulation of the environment around them was subtle and complete in a fashion we cannot understand. At least as yet. They played with atoms as an ordinary child plays with dominoes.

(What do you mean, "as yet"?)

Martin has assured me that we will. This is part of his

mission. First we must find the several selves we each contain, reconcile them, and then we will be ready for them, for the final step in the long evolution from the cave.

(Do you hear, Inquisitor? This business of finding the several selves within one's self. Isn't this what happened to Martin's interrogator?)

(Perhaps, perhaps. The man thought somehow that there was another in the room with him when he taped the narco-interview. He spent hours speaking with this person and answering. Only there was just one and he could not face that. After his personality degenerated, we of course . . .)

(Of course. . . .)

Although our mountains had been badly despoiled in the past, I was able to take Martin among them and show him something of the joy we had in nature, in the trees and the small things that creep through the brush, and in the hard and glittering rocks that made up our world. I took him among the Cherokees and the remains of the Iroquois and the Sioux and all the other tattered remnants of once-great races that you had herded into this tiny area. From Them he learned much. From us the sense of oneness with nature, from the Iroquois the ancient dream therapy that looks obliquely into a man's soul—the dream therapy that took your own western scientists centuries to discover long after it was a part of their culture.

We went down into the valley one day, where the streams wind sluggishly through tortuous channels from the mountains. I showed him how to pan the streams and we recovered tiny glints of fire, of garnets and rubies, that in another day would have been priceless. I told him of the time centuries before when a great house called Tiffany's had mined this area for the precious stones. Now there are only the small fragments in the stream, but their fire and inner nature pleased him. As we talked, he assembled an astonishing mound of the bright stones, none of them over a millimeter in length and then he sat gazing at them.

When I asked him what he was doing, he remarked that he was simply playing. He was still very much a child, you see. He frowned and the mound of stones moved uncertainly, then more certainly and then arose as a cloud of dull red. It formed a man image, then a woman image (for he was beginning to be troubled by this aspect of his humanness), and the shape caught the energy from some source and emitted the purest of reds so that the woman shape was a cloud of brilliant ruby light.

(Humph, laser phenomenon, no doubt. Can he really do this without apparatus?)

(It would seem so, Inquisitor.)

(More likely an excellent example of simple hypnotic positive illusion. I don't believe in such nonsense as this.)

We grew close, Martin and me. He had a remarkable capacity for friendship, even though he was remarkably naive about the world. He talked endlessly with the elders of all the tribes, absorbing their lore and their knowledge of the outside world. One day he asked me what it meant to be a blood brother.

"It's an old custom among many of the tribes," I said.

"I don't understand its meaning," he said.

"When two men are friends and feel their destinies are forever entwined, they mingle their blood and become one."

"This I understand," he said. For a moment the memories of what had happened earlier in the village troubled me, but he pressed those memories back into the deepest part of my mind as he and the children had done before. It was obvious that we were not ready for the horror that to them was the most ordinary part of their life and their passing on.

"You and I will become blood brothers, John," he announced that evening.

"I would like that," I said.

We sat in the light of the lantern in my cabin and each of us gashed our wrists so that the blood flowed freely. Then we crossed the wounds and watched the blood intermingle, vowing eternal friendship in the old manner. I watched his expression and saw a wonder come into his eyes, a sudden realization. At the same time my own mind was suddenly awash with the most conflicting sensations, as though I were simultaneously in a hundred bodies.

"Of course," he said. "It should have been easy to do it this way all along."

Before I could stop him, he raised my wounded wrist and began to deepen the wound until the blood spurted forth. I watched with a kind of horror as he did the same to his. We sat, two huddled male figures, while he raised my wrist to his mouth and signalled for me to do the same. I was suddenly frightened and dizzy but I did as he asked. We sat and silently drank each other's blood.

(The creature is mad. Disgusting. A stink in the nostrils of the Anointed Plurality.)

(Wait, Inquisitor Jarvis. Wait.)

In the end he caused the wounds to close. I do not know how he did this yet, but the knowledge is in my mind. Just as everything else is in my mind. Just as Martin is in my mind and I in his.

(Madness. This is clearly impossible.)

No, no, for as Martin said, no personality, no ego was lost in the ship. But the creatures of the ship needed food and here, except for the cities, food is more plentiful. The transfer is still important, however, and in our ritual Martin found the way that replaced their earlier cannibalism. It was a discovery of vast significance, he informs me.

(When did he till you that?)

Just this instant.

(Never mind this errant mysticism. Tell us about the last day.)

The last day before your people came to attack the alien ship and take Martin away, we went badger trapping. The badgers had returned to the hills in recent years and often provided a welcome change to our larder. We had once tried to hunt them with dogs, although our lore told us that this was not possible. The razor-clawed animal would roll on its back and rip at the underside of the poor dogs before disappearing into its hole. We lost many fine animals before we learned that they were best trapped.

We set green willow snares, Martin and I, in the old way. The snares were so arranged that, when the animal came to eat the bait, a split green-willow bow was triggered and closed on its leg. Even then this is not the surest way of trapping the beasts for they are fierce and want freedom above all else, preferring even death to capture. We can admire them for that for this is what we would have. Better freedom than the soul-destroying captivity of your Holy State.

(There is no question of it. He is a complete revanchist. Even though we have given our word that the tribes will not be molested, this one is destined for the Fields. Can you imagine such attitudes unleashed among the laity.?)

(They would not understand it, Inquisitor, any more than I do. The complete acceptance of our Holy State is a part of our life, a necessary outgrowth of the serum that had stifled all combativeness in our race.)

(A Combativeness and aggression that brought us once to racial extinction, Citizen.)

(I do not question it. Together we make a whole greater than its parts now. We are one with the State and the State is us without reservation and without flaw.)

(So be it.)

(So be it.)

The badger gnawed its leg off.

(John, what do you mean?)

The badger we had trapped gnawed its leg off. This is a common thing with them. They thrash at the trap, struggle so violently that sometimes they break bones. In the end if they cannot escape otherwise, they gnaw through their living flesh to gain release and crawl off into the brush to die. That was what happened with our trap. We came upon it, and the grass and kudzu vines were a mass of dull red blood. There in the green willow trap was the hind leg of the beast, tattered shreds of flesh still clinging to the bloody part where the beast had painfully torn its own leg off. The agony it must have suffered in its desire for freedom.

We followed the trail of blood. It was comparatively easy for the creature was bleeding its life away as it dragged itself from the trap. Over a hundred yards away, half-buried under a low scrub pine we found it. How it had made it that far, I don't know, a tribute to its brute heart. It lay with its muzzle bared, those white foam-speckled teeth screaming out its rage and its defiance even in death. The talons were unsheathed and for a moment it seemed as if it were ready to attack. Only it was quite dead.

Martin stood for a long time and looked at the pitiful creature. Then he said, "It wasn't truly free for it was returning to its own kind. It is only free of us."

"That is so," I said.

"But all humans on this planet are all bound in this fashion, one to the other, trapped as the beast was trapped by your trap. They are prisoners of a State that has bound them soul and mind and now they must be released from this trap so that they can find a new meaning, a new being. There will be those who will not survive the ordeal. Like this poor thing, they will gnaw their legs free of the trap and, before they can find help, they will crawl away and die."

He paused and thought for a long time. "Yes," he said at last, "it is better to crawl away and die than to resign oneself to the trap."

After that we returned in time to see your forces attack the ship in all their fury. It took them a long time to gather courage, and when they finally destroyed the ship and rounded up the children, Martin was among them. He warned them that this was not the end, that the ship was only one of many. Still, they took him away—for interrogation, they said—and the troops and war machines invested the village against all provisions of the treaty.

(That was the way it was, Citizen. I myself was one of the board of elders that ordered the attack. We knew we had to destroy the ship. I suppose we knew that there would be others, but the ship had to be destroyed. Especially after we received intelligence on what the children were doing in the village.)

(Was it necessary to kill the children?)

(Do you question it? We had one, Martin, for interrogation. We had no need of the others and we found that they were dangerous and could not be imprisoned.)

It is not as easy to kill us as you might imagine, Inquisitor. You destroy the physical bodies but the personalities of such as we are infectious. Like some amoeboid organism, we breed and spread and become a part of others.

(John Talltrees? . . .)

No, Inquisitor, it is not he.

(Shut up. I will not believe it.)

Martin still exists. He left your interrogator after giving him the gift of special insight. It was not Martin's fault that the interrogator was unable to reconcile his diverse personalities, that he became insane. Some of you will not and you will, of course, not survive. All of you must go through this evolution to rid yourselves of the influence of your State before you find that higher insight that Martin will bring you.

(What happened in the village?)

It is the end product of a million years of evolution.

(What happened an hour ago in the village?)

I can see it from here. We are, after all, only a few miles from the village. I sense that we are in one of your mobile interrogation vans. Surely, from this short a distance you must have seen?

(What happened in the village?)

They came from the sky. They knew that one of Their ships had been destroyed and now They knew the true menace represented by us. They might have gone from this system and found a new home in peace. Now They know that They must stand and wipe out the very menace They created. In the end, of course, we will prevail and They will be a part of us.

(What happened in the village? John, John.)

I am John. Through Martin's eyes I saw the thing come out of the sky. It was even bigger than the one that had crashed before. It stretched over half the horizon and it came in with raging energies that caused the very mountains to flow. The pines burst into flames and feathered into charcoal. The pitiful few animals of the hills fled before it and were charred in turn. Then the village and all my people . . . all my people . . . all my people. . . .

(What about the troops?)

They are no more. Only Martin at a distance and I here remain. Martin, whom I taught friendship and who must go on, seeking new growth, new power until. . . .

(Inquisitor Jarvis, that sound.)

(No, They could not detect us.)

Hide, do what you will, They are determined to eliminate this infection.

(Sounds of hissing, falling structures, silence, then. . . .)

(Ohhh.)

(John, are you still there?)

Yes, I am here. We are here.

(The Citizen Interrogator is dead.)

It is unfortunate.

(Damn you and your cold acceptance of all this. Don't you realize your own race is in deadly danger?)

Martin has told me so.

(Where is he?)

He went elsewhere. But a part of him remains here.

(Damn his soul, damn his soul.)

Why are you crying?

(My world, my ordered secure world, the Holy State and its Faithful. What have he and his creatures done to my world?)

They will make it anew, now that they are joined.

(No, no, I will not have it. He may have escaped but I will find him, track him down, kill him. . . .)

Send him to the Fields?

(Kill him, kill him with all the implacable rage of the badger you trapped.)

Gnaw off your leg, Inquisitor? Will you gnaw off your leg? Is this the way to freedom?

(Damn you, I have the power to. . . .)

Kill me.

(Kill you.) (Silence.)

(John, John, I am a just man, hard but just.)

(I am not a cruel man. John!)

(Oh, God in Heaven, why did I do that?)

Anne McCaffrey

KILLASHANDRA-
CRYSTAL SINGER

KILLASHANDRA came in from the Milekey Mountains with a load of rose quartz prisms and cylinders in A-sharp or higher. She worked well in the upper registers, which gave her a distinct advantage over most of the crystal singers in the Heptite Guild.

When she'd hit the frequencies, holding the tone long enough to locate and pitch the crystal cutter, she hadn't thought twice before she'd decided shape: prisms and cylinders. A good crystal singer has to have, first of all, perfect pitch and then a fine intuition for shape. No sense coming in with black quartz in octagons and cubes when the critical demand was for beads and cones.

When Guildmaster Lanzecki told her she'd hit the market at the top, she shrugged.

"Made it lucky this time," she said, wincing as she remembered the last week on the Range. The sun had been fierce on the scars of her cuttings, half-blinding her, and the scream of crystal had sliced through her mind as she'd cut. But she'd been desperate to hack enough cargo to get off-world for awhile away from crystal song, far away, so her mind would have a chance to heal. "What's the guild's percentage of it?"

Lanzecki peered up at her from his console, a little smirk bending the left corner of his thin mouth.

"Don't quibble, Killashandra."

She bridled, knowing what he meant. "I'm one of the best

and you know it. I've got years to go." Her tithe to the guild would keep her when crystal had blown her mind and stopped her ears.

Lanzecki lifted one shoulder. "You've cut crystal a long time, Killashandra."

"I don't need reminders," she said, snapping the words out. And that was a fallacy for crystal singing sapped your memory. "How much is guild cut? I have to have enough to get off-world this time."

Lanzecki inclined his head slightly for the wisdom of that. "Yes, you've solo-ed too long. That's not smart, 'specially in the Milekeys. Find yourself a new partner off-world."

Killashandra laughed. "That's what you always say."

Lanzecki waggled a finger at her. "I mean it. You've been too damned lucky but I wouldn't cut my margins again so fine if I were you, not at your age, and not cutting solo."

She couldn't think what he meant. She'd always had a second sense for storms in the Milekeys and always got out well in advance.

"You missed a big one by two hours and *that* is close," Lanzecki told her.

"Close but I can still scramble. How many machs did it reach?" she asked with a good show of indifference, considering the cold fear in her belly. She couldn't remember storm-sign.

Lanzecki tapped out the proper sequence and the slides on the back wall altered swiftly until the Milekey Range and a weatherscope were superimposed. The disturbance had reached the frightening velocity of twelve, mach forces that would have blown her mind had she been caught among crystal.

"There'll be good cutting when I go back," she said with an arrogant smile. No one else could cut rose quartz true in the Milekeys.

"Just don't go back solo, Killa." Lanzecki was completely serious. "You've sung crystals a long time now. You pulled out with a crazy two-hour margin but one day you'll stay just that moment too long and poff. . . ." He threw his hands up, fingers wide. "Burst ears and scrambled brains."

"That's the time, my friend," and Killashandra patted the console on which he had just recorded her tithe, "I get some of my own back."

Lanzecki eyed her. "With your ears ruptured and your mind rocking? Sure, Killa. Sure. Look, there're half a dozen good men'd double you anytime you raised your finger. A good duet makes more than a solo. Larsdahl. . . ."

"Larsdahl?" Killashandra was scornful and suspicious.

"You two worked damned well together."

"Lanzecki, how much did he slip you to remind me of him?"

Lanzecki's thin face became absolutely expressionless. When he spoke again, his voice was hard, as if he regretted his impulse.

"I was wrong, Killashandra. It's too late for you to cut duo. Crystal's in your soul." He turned away.

She waited a moment, trying to be amused by his accusation. As if she'd ever sing duet with Larsdahl again. Then she wondered why. There must have been a good reason once if Lanzecki said they'd worked well together once. He'd know. But the prohibition against Larsdahl must have been severe for it to stay so firmly in her mind, even if she couldn't remember the details.

She decided to clean up and outfit in her guild room. She must have something wearable left from her last trip in. Not that she could remember that time particularly well. That was one problem with being a crystal singer: The sonics did something to your recall circuits. Well, that was one excuse. Actually, unless you went off-world completely, and got away from crystal, nothing memorable ever happened.

Maybe she should double again. "Crystal in her soul, indeed!" Why *had* she split with Larsdahl? Why had he prejudiced her against any desire to share anything? And he'd had the nerve, the gall, the double-juice to ask about her? She snorted, wondering if he still sang slightly sharp. It'd been the devil to compensate when they cut minor notes.

She felt exhausted as she thumbed the lock on the door to her room and her body still pulsed with the frequencies of the Milekey lodes. She punched for a radiant bath, stripping as she heard the viscous liquid plunging into the tub-tank. Once immersed in that, the fatigue—and the resonances—would drain from her body and she could think beyond the next note.

By then, she did remember patches of her last break. They didn't please her. For one thing, she'd come in with a light load, forced off the Range a few kilos ahead of a bad storm. She'd reaped the benefits of that storm this trip, of course; that was the way of it with crystals. But she hadn't had enough credit to get offplanet. (If a singer worked one lode a long while, those crystals had the power to call and resonate you no matter where you were on Ballybran until you *had* to go back to them.) She'd been tired, and lonely and sought company in a landsman; tone-deaf, sober-sided so she couldn't circe him. But he hadn't been man enough to anneal her. "Crystal in my soul, indeed!" Lanzecki's words stung, like crystal scratch.

She made a noise of sheer self-disgust and pulled herself from the tank. The radiant fluid sheeted from her body, as firm and graceful as a youngster's. Killashandra puzzled idly on the matter of personal chronology. She couldn't remember her approximate age; it usually never mattered to a crystal singer. Something about the sonics, the crystal songs, stimulated the regenerative RNA and a crystal singer looked and felt young for far longer periods of time than other mortals. Not immortality, but close to it. The price was the risk of numb ears and scrambled brains, high enough.

"This time I'll be off-planet," she told her reflection and slid open the dresser panel.

She was mildly surprised at the finery there and decided she must have spent what credit she'd had for pretty threads to lure that unwary landsman. He'd been a brute of a lover, though a change. Anything had been a change from the possessiveness of Larsdahl. How dare he inquire after her? There was no harmony between them any more. He had no lien or hold on her because they'd *been* a duet!

Angrily Killashandra punched for Port Authority and inquired the destinations of imminent blast-offs.

"Not much, C. S. Killashandra," she was told politely. "A

small freighter is loading for the Armagh system. . . ."

"Have I been there?"

Pause. "No, ma'am."

"What does Armagh do for itself?"

"Exports fish oils and glue," was the semi-disgusted reply.

"Water world?"

"Not total. Has the usual balance of land and ocean. . . ."

"Tropical?"

"It has a very pleasant tropical zone. All water sports, tasty foods if you like a high fruit/fish diet."

"Book me." Crystal singers could be high-handed, at least on Ballybran.

"Blast-off at 2230 today," Port Authority told her.

"Grand." And Killashandra broke the connection.

She drew on the soberest garments in the press, randomly selected half a dozen, tossed them into a vapak, and closed it. She hesitated, mid-room, glancing about incuriously. It was, of course, the standard member room, and sterile. No trace of anything personal, of Killashandra.

"Because," Killashandra said out loud as if her voice might at least be imprinted on the room, "I'm nothing but a crystal singer with only a present to live in."

She slammed the door as she left but it didn't do much to satisfy her discontent.

She had time to get the refracting lenses removed from her eyes. It didn't change her outlook much. In fact, Ballybran looked duller than usual as she flitted to the Port Authority Terminal. She left the flit for any other crystal singer who might need transport from the terminal. She remembered at the last to punch through to the Guild Hall and give her off-planet destination. And she withdrew her priority rights on the Milekey lode until her return. If someone, and she felt it would be Larsdahl, wanted to try their luck there, they could for all of her. They might even make a good haul, now that the latest storm had changed the frequencies again.

Briefly her body ached for those resonances, for the dazzle of rainbow light prisms dancing off variegated quartz, for the pure sweet sound of crystal waking in the early morning sun, or sighing in the cold virginal light of one of the larger moons, for the subsonic hum that ate through bone in black cold night.

Then she dealt with the formalities of lifting off-world and settling in her cabin.

She entered the common room for the first time the third day out, having enjoyed a deep drug-sleep to purge the last of crystal sound from her blood and bone. She was hungry, for more than food, a hunger she could keep leashed as far as she herself was concerned. But the eight male passengers and the two crewmen who circulated in the transit territory were affected by her sensuality. There wasn't anyone she wanted so she retired to her cabin and remained there the rest of the trip.

Armagh III's Port Authority Terminal smelled of fish oil and glue. Great casks were being trundled into the hold of the freighter as she bade an impatient farewell to the passenger steward. She flashed her general credentials and was admitted unconditionally to the planet as a leisure guest. No problem so she hadn't had to use her guild membership. Armagh III was an open planet.

She rented a flit and checked into the Touristas for a list of resorts. It was too lengthy and so she closed her eyes, and bought a ticket to the destination on which her finger settled: Trefoil, on the southeastern coast. She paused long enough to obtain a quick change of Armagh clothing, bright patterns in a lightweight porous weave, and was off.

Trefoil was small, a fishing town. Ships under sail were tacking across the harbor. She thought she'd seen sailships before but, of course, she couldn't be sure. Her curiosity roused, she sauntered down to the docks to watch a huge two-master beat up the channel to the wharves, its crew bustling about the decks, which glinted with an almost crystalline sheen.

"What makes the decks shine?" she asked another observer.

"Fish oils," was the somewhat terse reply and then the man, a red-bearded giant, took a second look. Men usually did at Killashandra. "First time on Armagh?"

Killashandra nodded, her eyes intent on the sailship.

"Been here long?"

"Just arrived."

"Got a pad?"

"No."

"Try the Golden Dolphin. Best food in town and best brewman."

Killashandra turned to look at him then. "You pad there?"

"How else could I judge?" the man replied with charming candor.

Killashandra smiled back at him, neither coldly nor invitingly. Neutral. He reminded her of someone. They both turned back to watch the docking ship.

Killashandra found the process fascinating and silently applauded the well-drilled crew: each man seemed to perform his set task without apparent instruction from the man in the bridge house. The big hull drifted slowly sideways toward the wharf. The sails flapped, empty of wind, and were quickly gathered and fastened along the booms. Two crewmen flung lines ashore, fore and aft; then leaped after them when the distance closed, flipping the heavy lines deftly around the bollards and snubbing the ship securely.

Armagh men ran to height, tanned skins, and strong backs, Killashandra noticed approvingly. Redbeard was watching her out of the corner of his eye. He was interested in her all right. Just then, the nearest sailor turned landside, and waved in her direction. His teeth were startlingly white against the mahogany of his skin. He tossed back a streaked blond curly mane of hair and waved again. He wore the long oil-shiny pants of his profession and an oddly fashioned vest, which left chest and arms bare and seemed stiff with double hide along the ribs. He looked incredibly muscular. Was he waving at her? No, at Redbeard beside her, who now walked forward to meet his friend. A third man, black-bearded and tangle-maned, joined them, was embraced by Redbeard. The trio stood, facing the ship, talking among themselves until a fearsome machine glided along rails to their side of the dock. It extruded a ramp out and down, onto the deck of the boat, where it hovered expectantly.

The two sailors had jumped back aboard, the blond man moving with the instinctive grace of the natural athlete so that the black-haired man looked clumsy in comparison. As a team, they heaved open the hatch. The hesitant ramp extruded clamps that fastened to the deck and the lip of the opened hold. More ramp disappeared into the maw of the ship. Moments later the ramp belt moved upward and Killashandra saw her first lunk, the great oil fish of Armagh, borne away on its last journey.

She became absorbed in the unloading process, which, for all the automated assistance of the machine, still required the human element. The oil scales of the huge fish did not always stay on the rough surface of the ramp belt and had to be forced back on manually. The blond used an enormous barbed hook, planting it deep in what was actually the very tough hide of the elusive fish and deftly flipping the body into place again. Redbeard seemed to have some official position for he made notes of the machine's dials, used the throat mike often, and seemed to have forgotten her existence entirely. Killashandra approved. A man should get on with his work.

Yes, especially when he worked with such laudable economy of motion and effort. Like the young blond.

In fact, Killashandra was rather surprised when the ramp suddenly retracted and the machine slid sideways to the next hold. A small barefoot rascal of a lad slipped up to the crewmen, a tray of hot pies balanced on his head. The aroma was tantalizing and Killashandra realized that she'd not eaten since breaking fast on the freighter that morning. Before she could signal the rascal to her, his merchandise had been bought up by the seaman. Irritated, Killashandra looked landward. The docks couldn't be dependent on the services of small boys. There must be other eating facilities nearby. There were, of course, but off-dock. With a backward glance at her blond sailor, contentedly munching from a pie in each hand, she left the wharf.

As it happened the eating house she chose displayed a placard advertising the Golden Dolphin. The hostelry was up the beach, set back amid a grove of frond-leaved trees, far enough around a headland from the town and the wharf so that commercial noise was muted. She took a room with a veranda looking out over the water. She changed into native clothing and retraced her steps along the quiet corridor to the public room.

"What's the native brew?" she asked the barman, settling herself on the quaint high wooden stool.

"Depends on your capacity, m'dear," the little black man told her, grinning a welcome.

"I've never disgraced myself."

"Tart or sweet?"

"Hmmm. Tart, cool, and long."

"There's a concoction of fermented fruits, native to this globe, called 'harmat.' Powerful."

"Keep an eye on me then, man. You call the limit."

He nodded respectfully. He couldn't know that a crystal singer had a metabolism that compensated for drug or narcotic or excess alcohol. A blessing-curse. Particularly if you were injured off-world, with no crystal around to draw the noise of accidental pain from your bones and muscles.

Harmat was tart, cool, and long, with a pleasant aftertaste that kept the mouth sweet and soothed the throat.

"A good drink for a sun world. And sailors."

"Aye it is," the barman said, his eyes twinkling. "And if it weren't for them, we could export more."

"I thought Armagh's trade was fish oils and glue."

The barman wrinkled his nose disdainfully. "It is. Harmat off-world commands a price, only trade rules say home consumption comes first."

"Invent another drink."

The barman frowned. "I try. Oh, I try. But they drink me dry of anything I brew."

"You're brewman as well?"

He drew himself up, straight and proud. "I gather the fruit from my own land, prepare it, press it, keg it, age it."

She questioned him further, interested in another's exacting trade, and thought if she weren't a crystal singer, brewmaking would have been fun.

Biyanco, for that was the brewman's name, chatted with her amiably—he was an amusing fellow—until the laughter and talk of a large crowd penetrated the quiet gloom of the public room.

"The fishermen," he told her, busying himself by filling glass after glass after glass of harmat, lining them up along the bar.

He was none too soon, for the wide doors of the public room swung open and a horde of oil-trousered, vested men and women surged up to the bar, dark hands closing on the nearest glass, coins spinning and clicking to the wooden surface. Killashandra remained on her stool but she was pressed hard on both sides by thirsty people who spared her no glance until they'd finished the first and were bawling for a refill. Then she was rather casually, she felt, dismissed as the fisherfolk laughed and talked trade.

"You'd best watch that stuff," said a voice in her ear and she saw Redbeard.

"I've been warned," she answered, grinning.

"Biyanco makes the best harmat this side of the canal. It's not a drink for the novice."

"I've been warned," she repeated, mildly amused at the half-insult. Of course, the man couldn't know she was a crystal singer. So his warning had been kindly meant.

A huge bronzed fist brushed past her left breast. Startled, she looked up into the brilliant blue eyes of the blond sailor, received an incurious appraisal that warmed briefly in the way a man will look at a woman, and then grew cautious.

Killashandra looked away first, disturbed and disappointed. He was much too young for her. She turned back to Redbeard, who grinned as if he had watched the swift exchange of glances and was somehow amused by it.

"I'm Thursday, Shamus Thursday, ma'am," the redbeard said.

"Killashandra is my name," she replied and extended her hand.

He couldn't have told her profession by her grip but the strength surprised him. She could see that. Killashandra was not a tall or heavily boned woman; crystal cutting does not need mass, only controlled energy and that could be developed in any arm.

"This is my good friend, Shad Tucker," and Thursday gestured to the blond.

Thankful that the press of bodies made it impossible for her to do the courteous handshake, Killashandra nodded to Shad Tucker.

"And my old comrade of the wars, Tir Donnell," Shamus Thursday motioned to the blackbeard, who also contented himself with a nod and grin at her. "You'd be here for a rest, Killashandra?" And when she nodded, "And why would you pick such a dull fisherman's world as Armagh if you'd all the galaxy to choose from?"

Killashandra had heard that sort of question before, how many times she didn't care to remember. She'd also heard the same charming invitation for confidence.

"Perhaps I like water sports," she replied, smiling back at him, and not bothering to hide her appraisal.

To her surprise, he threw back his head and laughed. She could see where he'd trimmed the hairs from his throat, leaving a narrow band of white flesh that never saw sun. His two buddies said nothing but their eyes were on her.

"Perhaps you do, ma'am. And this is the place. Did you want the long wave ride? There's a boat out every dawn." Shamus looked at her questioningly. "Then water skating? Submarining? What *is* your pleasure, elusive Killashandra?"

"Rest. I'm tired."

"Oh, I'd never think you'd ever known fatigue, ma'am!" The expression in his eyes invited her to confide.

"For someone unfamiliar with the signs, how would you know?"

"She's got you there, Shamus," said Tir Donnell, clapping his friend on the shoulder. Shad Tucker smiled, a sort of shy, amused smile, as if he hadn't suspected her capable of caustic reply, and wasn't sure he should enjoy it at his friend's expense.

Shamus grinned, shrugged, and eyed Killashandra with respect. Then he bawled to Biyanco that his glass had a hole in it.

When the edge of their thirst had been satisfied, most of the fishermen left. "In search of other diversion," Shamus said but he, Tir Donnell, and Shad Tucker merely settled stools around her and continued to drink.

She matched them, paid her rounds, and enjoyed Shamus' attempts to pry information, any personal information, from her.

He was not, she discovered, easily put off, nor shy of giving facts about himself or his friends. They'd all worked the same fishing boat five seasons back, leaving the sea periodically as the monotony or bad fishing turned them off temporarily. Shamus had an interest in computers and often did wharfman's chores if the regular men were away when ships came in. Tir Donnell needed some ready credit, was working the lunk season and would return to his regular job inland. Shad Tucker, the only off-worlder, had sailed the seas of four planets before he was landed on Armagh.

"Shad keeps saying he'll move on, but he's been here five years and more, and no sign of applying for a ticket-off," Shamus told Killashandra.

Tucker only shrugged, the slight tolerant smile playing at the corner of his mouth, as if chary of admitting even that much about himself.

"Don't let Shad's reticence mislead you, ma'am," Shamus went on, laying a hand on his friend's shoulder. "He's accredited for more than a lunk fisher. Indeed he is. Got mate's tickets on four water worlds that make sailing Armagh look like tank bathing. Came here with a submariner rig one of the Anchorite companies was touting." He shrugged, eloquently indicating that the company's praise had fallen on deaf Armaghan ears.

"They're tradition bound on Armagh," Tucker said, his accent a nice change, soft on her ears. She had to sharpen her hearing to catch what he said. Shamus' light baritone was almost harsh by contrast.

"How so?" she asked Shad, ignoring what Shamus started to say.

"They feel there is one *good* way to catch lunk when it's in oil. By net. That way you don't bruise the flesh so much and the lunk doesn't struggle the way he does on a hook and sour the oil. The captains, they've a sense of location that doesn't need sonic gear. I've sailed with five or six of the best and they always know when and where the lunk are running. And how many they can bring from that deep.''

And, thought Killashandra, bemused by Shad's soft accent, *you'd give your arm to develop that sense.*

"You've fished on other worlds?'' she asked out loud.

"Aye.''

"What, for instance?'' He was as elusive with information as a fish. Or herself.

"Oh, spiderfish, crackerjaw, bluefin, skaters, and Welladay whales.''

The young man said it casually, as if encounters with such aquatic monsters were of no account. Shamus' eyes were alight, as if he had accurately gauged the effect of that catalog on Killashandra.

"A crackerjaw opened his back for him on Spindrift,'' Shamus said, proudly. "And he flew five miles with a skater and brought him down, the largest one ever recorded on Mandalay.''

Killashandra wasn't sure why Shamus Thursday wished to extol his friend. But it made him more acceptable in her eyes. Shad was too young, anyhow. Killashandra made no further attempt to draw Shad out but turned to Tir Donnell and Shamus.

Despite a continued concern for her consumption of harmat, Shamus kept ordering until full dark closed abruptly down on the planet and the artificial lights came on in the room.

"Mealtime,'' Biyanco announced in a loud, penetrating voice and activated a barrier that dropped over the bar. He appeared through a side door and briskly gestured them to a table for four on the other side of the room. Killashandra made no resistance to Shamus' suggestion that they all dine together and she spent the rest of the evening in their company. And her night alone. By choice. She'd not made up her mind.

When the sun came up over the edge of the sea, she was down in the hotel's private lagoon, floating on the buoyant waters, just as the lunk ships, sails fat with dawn winds, slid out to open sea with incredible speed.

To her surprise, Shamus appeared at midday and offered to show her Trefoil's few diversions. Nothing loath, she went and found him most agreeable company, conversant on every phase of Trefoil's domestic industry. He steered her from the usual tourist paths, for which she was grateful. She abhorred that label though that was, in essence, her status on any world but Ballybran. Nor did she give Shamus Thursday any hint of her profession despite all his attempts to wheedle the information from her.

It wasn't exactly that she liked being secretive, but few worlds understood the function of crystal singers and some very odd habits and practices had been attributed to them. Killashandra had learned discretion and caution, and remembered them.

Late afternoon and a bleeper on Shamus' belt alerted him to return to the dock, the fishing boats had been sighted.

"Sorry, m'dear," he said as he executed a dipping turn of his fast flipper. "Duty calls."

She elected to join him on the wharf, allowing him to think it was his company she preferred. Actually she wanted to watch the silent teamwork of docking, and see the mahogany figure of Shad Tucker in action. He was much too young for her, she told herself again, but a right graceful person to observe.

They'd had a quick plenteous catch that day, Killashandra was told as the fishermen drowned their thirsts in harmat at the Golden Dolphin. Tucker seemed unusually pleased and Killashandra could not resist asking why.

"He's threatening to buy a ticket-off," Shamus told her when Shad replied with an indolent shrug. "But he won't go. He never does. He's been here five years, longer that on any other planet."

"Why?" Killashandra asked Shad, then had to hush Shamus. "Let Tucker reply. He knows his own mind, doesn't he?"

Shad regarded her with mild surprise and the indolent look left his blue eyes, replaced by an intentness she found hard to ignore.

"This is a real sea world," Shad said, picking his words in his soft-accented way, "not some half-evolved plankton puddle."

He doesn't open his lips wide enough to enunciate properly, she thought, and wondered why he guarded himself so.

"You've lunk for profit, territ and flatfish for fine eating, the crustaceans and bivalves for high livers, then the sea fruits for a constant harvest. Variety. I might buy myself a strip of land and stay."

"You do ship on more than the lunk boats?"

Shad was surprised at her question. "All the boats fish lunk when it runs. Then you go after the others."

"If you've a mind for drudgery," said Tir Donnell gloomily.

Shad gave Tir a forebearing glance. "Lunk requires only muscle," he said with a sly grin.

This appeared to be an old challenge, for Tir launched into a debate that Shad parried with the habit of long practice.

For the sake of being perverse, Killashandra took Tir Donnell to bed that night. She didn't regret the experience although there was no harmony between them. His vehemence did take the edge off her hunger if it gave her no peace. She did not encourage him to ask for more. Somewhere, long ago, she'd learned the way to do that without aggravating a lover.

He was gone by dawn. Shamus dropped by a few hours later and took her to see a sea-fruit farm on the peninsula, ten kilometers from Trefoil to the south. When she assured Max Ennert, the farmer, of her depth-worthiness, they all fitted out with breather tanks and went submarine.

Enclosed by water, isolated by her trail of bubbles, though attached by guideline to Max and Shamus, Killashandra realized—probably for an uncountable time—why crystal singers sought water worlds. Below sea level, there was insulation against aural sound, relief from the play of noise against weary eardrums.

They drifted inches above the carefully tended sea gardens, Max and Shamus occasionally pruning off a ripe frond of grape or plum, shoving them in the net bags they towed. They by-passed reapers in a vast sea-valley where weed was being harvested. Occasionally loose strands would drift past them, the fuller longer ones deftly caught and netted by the men.

Killashandra was content to follow, slightly behind Max, slightly ahead of Shamus, craning her neck, angling her body to enjoy as much of the clear sea-view as possible. One or the other man checked her gauges from time to time. Euphoria could be a curse under sea and they didn't know her capacity, nor the professional immunity she enjoyed.

Perhaps that was why Shamus argued with Max at one point, when they'd been below some two hours. They stayed down almost three more before they completed the circuit. As they walked out of the sea at Max's landing, night was approaching with the usual tropical dispatch.

"Stay on, Shamus, Killashandra, if you've no other plans," Max said but the words sounded rehearsed, strained.

She entered the room where she had changed to sea-dress and heard Shamus' footsteps right behind her. She didn't bother closing the door. He did, and had her in his arms the next instant. She made no resistance to his advance, nor did she respond. He held her from him, surprised, a question in his eyes.

"I'm not susceptible to euphorics, Shamus," she told him.

"What are you talking about?" he asked, eyes wide with innocence.

"And I've submarined on more worlds than Shad has sailed."

"Is it Tucker you're after?" He didn't seem jealous, merely curious.

"Shad's . . ." and she shrugged, unwilling to place the young man in any category.

"But you don't fancy me?" Not aggrieved, again, merely curious.

She looked at him a long moment. "I think . . . ." she began, pausing as she voiced an opinion that had been subconscious till that moment, ". . . you remind me too much of someone I've been trying to forget."

"Oh, just remind you?" Shamus' voice was soft and coaxing, almost like Tucker's. She put that young man firmly out of her mind.

"Not to worry, Shamus. The resemblance is purely superficial."

His eyes twinkled merrily and Killashandra realized that the resemblance had been indeed purely superficial, for the other man would have responded with dark suspicion and urgent questions she'd have left unanswered purely to annoy him more.

"So, dark and mysterious lady, when you get to know me better. . . ."

"Let me get to know you better first."

They flitted back to Trefoil, circling over quays empty of any fishing craft.

"Lunk is moving offshore," Shamus said. "Season's about over, I'd say."

"Does Tucker have enough for a ticket-off?"

"I wouldn't know." Shamus was busy landing. "But Tir needs one more good haul. And so, I suspect, does Skipper Garnsey. They'll track school as far as there's trace before they head in."

Which was the substance of the message left for Shamus at the Golden Dolphin. So Killashandra, Shamus, and Biyanco talked most of the evening with damned few other drinkers at the bar.

That was why Killashandra got an invitation to go with Biyanco fruit-harvesting. "Land fruit for harmat," Biyanco said with an odd shudder.

Shamus laughed and called him an incorrigible lubber. "Biyanco swears he's never touched sea-fruit in his life."

"Never have been that poor," Biyanco said with some dignity.

The brewman roused her before dawn, his tractor purring outside her veranda. She dressed in the overall he'd advised and the combi-boots, and braided her hair tightly to her skull on the outward leg of their trip.

Trefoil nestled on the curved sands of a giant horseshoe bay, foothills at its back. Rain forests that were all but impenetrable swept up the hills, sending rank streamers across the acid road in vain attempts to cover that man-made tunnel into the drier interior.

Biyanco was amiable company, quiet at times, garrulous but interesting at others. He stopped off on the far side of the first range of foothills for lorries and climbers. None of the small boys and girls looked old enough, Killashandra thought, to be absent from schooling. All carried knives half again as long as their legs from sheaths thong-tied to their backs. All wore the coveralls and combi-boots with spurred clamp-ons for tree-climbing.

They chattered and sang, dangling their legs from the lorries as the tractor churned through the acid road. Occasionally one of them would wield his knife, chopping an impertinent streamer that clasped itself to a lorry.

Biyanco climbed farther above sea level by the winding acid road until he finally slowed down, peering at the roadside. Five kilometers later he let out an exclamation and veered the tractor to the left, his hands busy with dials and switches. A warning hoot brought every climber's legs back into the lorries. Flanges, tilting downward, appeared along the lorry loadbeds and acid began to drip from this shield. Acid sprayed out, arcing well past the tractor's leading edge, dissolving vegetations. Suddenly the tractor's treads locked and ground on metal. Biyanco pushed a few toggles, closed a switch, and suddenly the tractor purred smoothly along the hidden track.

"Own this side of the mountain, you know," Biyanco said, glancing at Killashandra to see the effect of his announcement. "Ah, you thought I was only a barman, didn't you? Surprised you, didn't I? Ha." The little man was pleased.

"You did."

"I'll surprise you more before the day is over."

Which he did, sprier than she'd ever thought him, and elated with his success. She was glad for his sake and somewhat puzzled on her own account. He was adept enough so that she ought to have enjoyed it, too. Was there crystal in her soul, after all? Was she too old to love?

They'd reached their destination, a permaformed clearing with acid-roofed buildings that housed his processing unit and temporary living quarters. The climbers he'd escorted went farther on, sending the lorries off on automated tracks, six climbers to each lorry. They'd evidently climbed for him before and in the teams they now assembled, for he gave a minimum of instruction before dismissing them to pick.

Then he'd shown Killashandra into the processing plant and explained the works succinctly.

Each of the teams worked a different fruit, he told her. The secret of good harmat lay in the careful proportions and blending of dead ripe fruit. There were as many blends of harmat as there were fish in the sea. His had made the Golden Dolphin famous; that's why so many Armaghans patronized the hostelry. None of this vapid, innocuous stuff came from his stills. Harmat took months to bring to perfection: the fruit he'd process today would not be fermented for nine months and would not be offered for sale for six years. Then he took her below ground, to the cool dark storage area, deep in the permaform. He showed her the automatic alarms if the vicious digger roots of the jungle ever penetrated the permaform, he wore a bleeper on his belt at all times (he never did remove the belt but it was made of soft tough fiber). He let her sample the brews and it amused her that he would sip abstemiously while filling her cup full. Because she liked him and she'd learned about harmat from him, she gradually imitated drunk.

He'd had a good deal of experience, Killashandra had to admit, and he tried his damnedest to bring her to pitch but the frequency was wrong, as it had been with Tir, would have been with Shamus, and this badly puzzled Killashandra. She ought not to have such trouble off-world.

While Biyanco slept, before the full lorries glided back to their clearing, she probed her patchy memory, again and again stopped by Larsdahl's cynical laugh. Damn the man! He was haunting her even on Armagh. He had no right to taint everything she touched, every association she tried to enjoy. She could remember, too, enough snatches to know that her previous break had been as disastrous. Probably other breaks, too. In the quiet cool dark of the sleeping room, Biyanco motionless with exhaustion beside her, Killashandra bleakly cursed Larsdahl. For he'd sworn she would find fulfillment with no other lover if she left his bed. Laughing, she'd left him, sure then of herself where she was completely unsure now. "Crystal in her soul?"

Experimentally she ran her hand down her bare body, to the

hard flesh of her thighs, the softness of her belly, her firm breasts. She'd had her children decades before, they'd be grown and parents. Maybe grandparents. You never conceived once you sang crystal. Small loss, she thought, and then, suddenly, wasn't sure.

Damn, damn! Damn Larsdahl. *She'd* found the Milekey lode. She had the priority right. He couldn't have mined it, he couldn't sing the right resonances, he didn't have the cutting skill for the light quartzes. She'd tried, grant her that, to show him but they'd crack, he simply hadn't the sense of pitch. At least for rose crystal. And then he'd withheld the gift of peace from her body because she wouldn't . . . because she couldn't . . . teach him her trick of pitch.

"You have it or you haven't, Larsdahl," she'd told him, implored him, shouted at him. "You can't be taught any more than you can teach crystal singing to the deaf! I can't help you!"

There'd been bitter recriminations, physical battles, because Larsdahl hadn't wanted to let her go even after he'd jeopardized their partnership with his insistence. She'd had to invoke guild protection, something a crystal singer ought not to have to do. But it had sobered Larsdahl and he'd let her alone. Not entirely alone: there'd be the odd message from another singer. Or, the verbal communication for Lanzecki to pass on. Lanzecki ought to know better.

And you didn't, damn it, need two to work her priority range. The sounds were too pure: two ears were better than four. Two bodies inhibited the purities, muddied the pitch. She'd learned that much from Larsdahl.

The sound of the returning lorries, the singing of the climbers, roused Biyanco. He blinked at her, having forgot in his sleeping that he'd taken a woman again. With solemn courtesy, he thanked her for their intercourse, and having dressed, excused himself with grave ceremony. At least a man had found pleasure in her body, she thought.

She bathed, dressed, and joined him as the full fruit bins began spilling their colorful contents into the washing pool. Biyanco was seated at the controls, his nimble fingers darting here and there as he weighed each bin, computed the price, and awarded each chief his crew's chit. It was evidently a good pick, judging by the grins on every face, including Biyanco's.

As each lorry emptied, it swiveled around and joined the line on the tractor that was also headed homeward. All were shortly in place and then the second part of the processing began. The climbers took themselves off under the shade of the encroaching jungle and ate their lunches.

Abruptly noise pierced Killashandra's ears. She let out a scream, stifling a repetition against her hand but not soon enough to escape Biyanco. The noise ceased. Trembling with relief, Killashandra looked around, astonished that no one else seemed affected by the appalling shriek.

"You are a crystal singer, then, aren't you?" asked Biyanco, steadying her as she rocked on her feet. "I'm sorry. I wasn't sure but I forgot the crystals in the drive have been off. Honest I did, or I'd have warned you." He was embarrassed and earnest.

"You should have them balanced," Killashandra replied angrily and immediately apologized. "How could you know I might be a crystal singer?"

Biyanco looked away from her now. "Things I've heard."

"What have you heard?"

He looked at her then, his eyes steady. "That a crystal singer can sound notes that'll drive a man mad. That they lure men to them, seduce them, and then kidnap 'em away to Ballybran and they never come back."

Killashandra smiled, a little weakly because her ears still ached. "What made you think I wasn't?"

"Me!" He jabbed at his chest with a juice-stained finger. "You slept with *me*."

She reached out and touched his cheek gently. "You are a good man, Biyanco, besides being the best brewman on Armagh. And I like you. But you should get those crystals balanced."

Biyanco glanced over at the offending machinery and grimaced, "The balancer's got a waiting list as long as Murtagh River," he said. "You look pale. How about a drink? Harmat'll help . . . oh, you are a witch," he added, chuckling as he realized that she couldn't've been as drunk as she'd acted. Then a smile tugged his lips across his face. "Ohho, you are a something, Killashandra of Ballybran. I should've spotted your phony drunk, and me a barman all these decades." He chuckled again. "Well, harmat'll help your nerves." He clicked his fingers at one of the climber chiefs and the boy scampered into the living quarters, back again in a trice with glasses and a flask of chilled harmat.

She drank eagerly, both hands on the glass because she was still shaky. The cool tartness was soothing, though, and she wordlessly held the glass out for a refill. Biyanco's eyes were kind and somewhat anxious. He knew what unbalanced crystalline shrieks did to the sensitive nerves of a singer.

"You've not been harmed by it, have you?"

"No. No, Biyanco, we're tougher than that. It was the surprise. I wasn't expecting you to have crystal-driven equipment. . . ."

He grinned slyly. "We're not backward on Armagh for all we're quiet and peaceful. " He leaned back from her, regarding her with fresh interest. "Is it true that crystal singers don't grow old?"

"There're disadvantages to that, my friend."

He raised his eyebrows in polite contradiction. But she only smiled as she steadily sipped the harmat until all trace of pain had eased from her nerves.

"You told me you've only a certain time to process ripe fruit. If you'll let me take the tractor down the rails past the first ridge . . . No. . . ." and she vetoed her own suggestion arriving at an impulsive alternative. "How long do you have before the pick sours?"

"Three hours, tops," and in Biyanco's widening eyes she saw incredulous gratitude as he understood her intention. "You wouldn't?" he said in a voiceless whisper.

"I could and I would. That is, if you've the tools I need."

"I've tools," and, as if afraid she'd renege, he propelled her toward the machine shed.

He had what she needed, but the bare minimum. Fortunately, the all important crystal saws and knives were still very sharp and true. With two pairs of knowledgeable hands (Biyanco had put the driver together himself when he updated the plant's machinery thirty years ago), it was no trick at all to get down to the crystals.

"They're in thirds," he told her needlessly.

"Pitch?"

"B-flat minor."

"Minor? For heavy work like this?"

"Minor because it isn't that continuous a load and minors don't cost what majors do," Biyanco replied crisply.

Killashandra nodded, accepting the oblique snub. She hit the B-flat and the crystal hummed sweetly in tune. So did the D. It was the E that was sour—off by a half-tone. She cut off the resonance before the sound did more than ruffle her nerves. With Biyanco carefully assisting her, she freed the crystal of its brackets, cradling it tenderly in her hands. It was a blue, from the Ghanghe Range, more than likely, and old, because the blues were worked out now.

"The break's in the top of the prism, here," she said, tracing the flaw. "The bracket may have shifted with vibration."

"G'delpme, I weighed those brackets and felted them proper. . . ."

"Not to worry, Biyanco. Probably the expansion coefficient differs in this rain forest enough to make even properly set felt slip. Thirty years they've been in? You worked well."

They decided to shift pitch down, which meant she had to recut all three crystals, but that way he'd have a major triad. Because she trusted him, she let him watch as she cut and tuned. She had to sustain pitch with her voice after she had warmed them enough to sing, but she could hold a true pitch long enough to place the initial, and all-important cuts.

It was wringing wet work, even with the best of equipment and in a moderate climate. She was exhausted by the time they reset the felted brackets. In fact, he elbowed her out of the way when he saw how her hands trembled.

"Just check me," he asked but she didn't need to. He was spry in more than one way. She was glad she'd tuned the crystals for him. But he was too old for her.

She felt better when he started the processer again and there was no crystal torture.

"You get some rest, Killashandra. This'll take a couple more hours. Why don't you stretch out on the tractor van seat? It's wide enough. That way you can rest all the way back to Trefoil."

"And yourself, Biyanco?"

He grinned like the old black imp he was. "I'm maybe a shade younger than you, crystal singer Killashandra. But we'll never know, will we?"

She slept, enervated by the pitching and cutting, but she woke when Biyanco opened the tractor door. The hinge squeaked in C-sharp.

"Good press," he said when he saw she was awake. Behind in the lorries, the weary climbers chanted to themselves. One was a monotone. Before he could get on her nerves, they'd reached the village. The lorries were detached and the climbers melted into the darkness. Biyanco and Killashandra continued on the acid road back to Trefoil.

It was close to dawn before they pulled up at the Golden Dolphin.

"Killashandra?"

"Yes, Biyanco?"

"I'm in your debt."

"No, for we exchanged favors."

He made a rude noise. And she smiled at him. "We did. But if you need a price, Biyanco, then it's your silence on the subject of crystal singers."

"Why?"

"Because I'm human, no matter what you've heard of us. And I must have that humanity on equal terms or I'll shatter one day among the quartz. It's why we have to go off-world."

"You don't lure men back to Ballybran?"

"Would you come with me to Ballybran?"

He snorted. "You can't make harmat on Ballybran."

She laughed for he had given the right answer to ease his own mind. The tractor moved off softly in first.

She slept the sun around and woke the second dawn refreshed. She lazed in the water, having been told by the pug-nosed host that the lunk ships were still out. Biyanco greeted her that noonday with pleasantries and no references to favors past, present, or future. He was old enough, that brewman, she thought, to know what not to say.

She wondered if she should leave Trefoil and flit around the planet. There'd be other ports to visit, other fishermen to snare in the net of her attraction. One of them might be strong enough, must be strong enough to melt the crystal in her. But she tarried and drank harmat all afternoon until Biyanco made her go eat dinner.

She knew the lunk boats were in even before the parched seamen came thronging up the beachroad, chanting their need. She helped Biyanco draw glasses against their demand, laughing at their surprise to see her working behind the bar. Only Shad Tucker seemed unamazed.

Shamus was there, too, with Tir Donnell, teasing her as men have teased barmaids for centuries. Tucker sat on a stool in the corner of the bar and watched her, though he drank a great deal of harmat to "unstick his tongue from the roof of his mouth."

Biyanco made them all go eat, to lay a foundation for more harmat, he said. And when they came back, they brought a squeeze box, a fiddle, two guitars, and a flute. The tables were stacked against the wall and the music and dancing began.

It was good music, too, true-pitched so Killashandra could enjoy it, tapping her foot to the rhythms. And they played until the musicians pleaded for a respite, and leaving their instruments on the bar, swept out to the cool evening beach to get a second wind.

Killashandra had been dancing as hot and heavy as any woman, partnered with anyone who felt like dancing, including Biyanco. Everone except Tucker, who stayed in his corner and watched . . . her.

When the others left to cool off, she wandered over to him. His eyes were a brighter blue in the new red-tan of his face. He was picking his hands now and again because the last of the lunks had an acid in their scales that ate flesh. And he'd had to grab some barehanded at the last.

"Will they heal?" she asked.

"Oh, sure. Be dry tomorrow. New skin in a week. Doesn't hurt." Shad looked at his hands impersonally and then went on absently sloughing off the dying skin.

"You weren't dancing."

The shy grin twisted up one corner of his mouth and he ducked his head a little, looking at her from the side of his eyes.

"I've done my dancing. With the fish the past days. I like to watch, anyhow."

He unwound himself from the stool to reach out and secure the nearest guitar. He picked a chord, winced so he didn't see her shudder at the discord. Lightly he plucked the strings, twisting the tuning knob on the soured G, adjusting the E string slightly, striking the chord again and nodding with approval.

Killashandra blinked. The man had perfect pitch.

He began to play, softly, with a style totally different from the raucous tempi of the previous musicians. His picking was intricate and the rhythm sophisticated, yet the result was a delicate shifting of pattern and tone that enchanted Killashandra. It was improvisation at its best, with the player as intent upon the melody he produced as his only audience.

The beauty of his playing, the beauty of his face as he played, struck an aching in her bones. When his playing ceased, she felt empty.

She'd been leaning toward him, perched on a stool, elbows on her knees, supporting her chin with cradled hands. So he leaned forward, across the guitar, and kissed her gently on the mouth. They rose, as one, Shad putting the guitar aside to fold her in his arms and kiss her deeply. She felt the silk of his bare flesh beneath her hands, the warmth of his strong body against hers and then . . . the others came pouring back with disruptive noise. The mood he had so delicately created was brutally torn apart.

As well, thought Killashandra, as Shamus boisterously swung her up to the beat of a rough dance. When next she looked over her shoulder, Shad was cornered and watching, the slight smile on his lips, his eyes still on her.

He is much much too young for me, she told herself, *and I am very fragile with too much living.*

The next day she nursed what must have been her first hangover. She'd tried hard enough to acquire one. She lay on the beach in the shade and tried not to move unnecessarily. Otherwise she'd ache and hurt. No one bothered her until midday; presumably everyone was nursing hangovers of their own. Then Shad's large feet stopped on the sand beside her pallet. Shad's big knees cracked as he bent over her and his peeling hand tipped back the wide hat she wore against sun glare.

"You'll feel better if you eat this," he said, speaking very softly. He held out a small tray with a frosted glass and a plate of fruit chips on it.

She wondered if he were enunciating with extra care for she understood every soft word, even if she resented the gist of them. She groaned and he repeated his advice. Then he put gentle hands on her, raising her torso so she could drink without spilling. He fed her, piece by piece as a man feeds a sick and fretful child.

She felt sick and she was fretful but, when all the food and drink were in her belly, she had to admit that his advice was sound.

"I never get drunk."

"Probably not. But you also don't dance yourself bloody-footed either."

Her feet were tender, come to think of it, and when she examined the soles, discovered blisters and myriad thin scratches.

Tucker sat with her all afternoon, saying little. When he suggested a swim, she complied and the lagoon water was cooler than she'd remembered, or maybe she was hotter for all she'd been lying in the shade.

When they emerged from the water, she felt human, even for a crystal singer. And she admired his straight tall body, the easy grace of his carriage, and the fineness of his handsome face. But he was much too young for her. She would have to try Shamus for she needed a man's favors again.

Evidently it was not Shad's intention that she find Shamus for he persuaded her that she didn't want to eat in the hostelry; that it would be more fun to dig for bivalves where the tide was going out, in a cove he knew of, a short walk away. It is difficult to argue with a soft-spoken man, who is taller than you by six inches, and can carry you easily under one arm . . . even if he is a century or so younger.

And it was impossible not to touch his silky flesh when he brushed past her to tend the baking shellfish, or when he passed her wine-steeped fruit chips and steam roots.

When he looked at her, sideways, his blue eyes darker now, reflecting the fire and the night, it was beyond her to resist his importunities.

She woke on the dark beach, before the dying fire, with his sleeping weight against her side. Her arms were wrapped around his right arm, her head cradled on the cup of his shoulder. Without moving her head, she could see his profile. And she knew there wasn't any crystal in her soul. She could still give . . . and receive. For all she sang crystal, she still possessed that priceless human quality, annealed in the fire of his youth.

She'd been wrong to dismiss him for what was a mere chronological accident, irrelevant to the peace and solace he brought her. Her body was exultant, renewed.

Her stretching roused him to smile with unexpected sweetness into her eyes. He gathered her against him, the vibrant strength of his arms tempered to tenderness for her slight frame.

"You crazy woman," he said, in a wondering voice as he lightly scrubbed her scalp with his long fingers and played with her fine hair. "I've never met anyone like you before."

"Not likely to again." Please!

He grinned down at her, delighted by her arrogance.

"Do you travel much?" he asked.

"When the mood strikes me."

"Don't travel for awhile."

"I'll have to one day. I've got to go back to work, you know."

"What work?"

"I'm a guild member."

His grin broadened and he hugged her. "All right. I won't pry." His finger delicately traced the line of her jaw. "You can't be as old as you make out," he said for she'd been honest enough earlier to tell him they were not contemporary.

She answered him now with a laugh but his comment brought a chill to her.

It couldn't have been an accident that he could relieve her, she thought, caressing his curving thigh. She panicked suddenly at the idea that, once tasted, she could not drink again and strained herself to him.

His arms tightened and his low laugh was loving to her ears. And their bodies fit together again as fully and sweetly in harmony as before. Yes, with Shad Tucker, she could dismiss all fear as baseless.

Their pairing-off was accepted by Shamus and Tir who had his ready credit now and was off to apply it to whatever end he'd had in mind. Only Biyanco searched her face and she'd shrugged and given the brewman a little reassuring smile. Then he'd peered closely at Shad and smiled back.

That was why he said nothing. As she'd known he wouldn't. For Shad Tucker wasn't ready to settle on one woman. Killashandra was an adventure to him, a willing companion for a man just finished a hard season's work.

They spent the days together as well, exploring the coastline in both directions from Trefoil, for Shad had a mind to put his earnings in land or sea front. She had never felt so . . . so vital and alive. He had a guitar of his own that he'd bring, playing for hours little tunes he'd make up when they were becalmed and had to take shelter in the shade of the sail from Armagh's biting noonday sun. She loved to look at him while he played; his absorption had the quality of an innocent boy discovering major Truths of Beauty, Music, and Love. Indeed, his face, when he caressed her to a fever pitch of love, retained that same youthful innocence and intent absorption. Because he was so strong, because his youth was so powerful, his delicate, restrained love-making was all the more surprising to her.

The days multiplied and became weeks but so deep was her contentment that the first twinge of uneasiness caught her unawares. She knew what it was, though: her body's cry for crystal song.

"Did I hurt you?" asked Shad for she was in his arms.

She couldn't answer so she shook her head. He began to kiss her slowly, leisurely, sure of himself. She felt the second brutal knock along her spine and twisted herself closer in his arms so he wouldn't feel it and she could forget that it had happened.

"What's wrong, Killashandra?"

"Nothing. Nothing that you can't cure."

So he did. But afterward, she couldn't sleep and stared up at the spinning moons. She couldn't leave Shad now. Time and again he'd worked his magic with her until she'd've sworn all crystal thought was purged. Until she'd even toyed with the notion of resigning from the guild. When crystal got too bad, she could tune sour crystal on Armagh. But she must stay with Shad. He held back fear, he brought her peace. She'd waited for a lover like Shad Tucker so long, she had the right to enjoy the relationship.

The next moment another spasm struck her, hard, sharp, fierce. She fought it though her body arched with pain. And she knew she couldn't resign. That she was being inexorably drawn back. And she did not want to leave Shad Tucker.

To him, she was a novelty, a woman to make love to . . . now . . . when the lunk season had been good and man needed to relax. But Killashandra was not the sort of woman he'd build a home for on his acres of sea-front. For her, she loved him: for his youth, for his absurd gentleness and courtesy; because, in his arms, she was briefly ageless.

The profound cruelty of her situation was driven home to her mind as bitterly as the next hunger pain for crystal sound.

It isn't fair, she cried piteously. *It isn't fair. I can't love him. It isn't fair. He's too young. He'll forget me in other loves. And I . . . I'll not be able to remember him.* That was the cruelest part.

She began to cry, Killashandra who had foresworn tears for any man half a century before when the harmony between herself and Larsdahl had turned discordant. Her weeping, soft as it was, woke Shad. He comforted her, lovingly and complicated her feelings for him by asking no questions at all. Maybe, she thought with the desperation of fearful hope, he isn't that young. He might want to remember me.

And, when her tears had dried on her face, he kissed her again, with an urgency that must be answered. And was, as fully and sweetly as ever.

The summons came two days later. Biyanco tracked them in the cove and told her only that she had an urgent message. She was grateful for that courtesy but she hated the brewman for bringing the message at all.

It was a guild summons all right; she had to go back and sing rose crystal. Implicit in the message was a guild warning: she'd been away too long from crystal. What crystal gave, it took away. She stared at her reflection in the glass panel of the message booth. Yes, crystal could take away her appearance of youthfulness. How long would Shad remember the old woman she would shortly become?

So she started out to say goodbye to him. Best have it done quickly and now! Then back to Ballybran and forgetfulness in the crystal song. She felt cold all over.

He was sitting by the lagoon, strumming his guitar, his face absorbed in a melody he'd composed for her. It was a pretty tune, one that stopped in the mind and woke you humming it the next day.

Killashandra caught back her breath: Shad had perfect pitch: he could come with her, to Ballybran. She'd train him herself to be a crystal singer.

"Don't," said Biyanco stepping to her side.

"Don't what?" she asked coldly.

"If you really love him, Killashandra, don't. He'll remember you this way. That's what you want, isn't it?"

It was, of course, because she wouldn't. So she stood there, beside Biyanco, and listened to Shad sing, watched the boyish absorption on his beloved face and let cruelty wash hope out of her.

"It never works, does it, Killashandra?" Biyanco asked gently.

"No." She had a fleeting recollection of Larsdahl. They'd met somewhere, off-world. Hadn't they? They must have. Had she been lured to Ballybran by some ageless lover? Perhaps.

Who knew? The difference was that now, she was old enough not to play the siren for crystal. Old enough to leave love while he was young, and still in love enough to remember her only as a woman.

"No one forgets you, Killashandra," Biyanco said, his eyes dark and sad, as she turned to leave.

"Maybe I can remember that much."

Gene Wolfe

THE DEATH OF HYLE

I have never been a religious man, and I am not a religious man now. I have known all my life—at least, since I was seven or eight, when I began to read my older brother Walter's chemistry books, and later the big, old, red-bound encyclopedias in my father's study—that this world of supposedly sentient matter, this world that appears (I ought to have said, appeared) so solid to my admittedly bemused eyes—eyes enchained by maya, as the Hindus have been telling us for four thousand years—is insubstantial as vapor. Not only because what we have self-indulgently called our too-solid flesh is (as it is) no more than a cosmos of crackling energy; and not only because that fiction we refer to as objective reality is (as it is) the creature of the very radiation by which we gauge it—and of our senses—a creation shaped too by the digital nature of our brains and by our minds' deplorable habit of overlaying all we see and hear and feel with what we anticipated perceiving, overlaying it, I say, before warping the whole to bring it in line with our past experiences; but most of all because it is the least substantial of the laws that rule us that tyrannize us most—so that we, every one of us, feel crushed beneath the dictum that one thousand less nine hundred and thirty is seventy, and tortured by the implacable commandment to destroy the thing we love, while the solid fact (as we call it) that Madagascar is off the eastern coast of Africa affects us not at all.

134

I am back again; though it must seem to you who read this that I was never gone, it had been a long time—several days at least. I gauge the time by the grass; there are no newspapers, no bottles of milk on our doorstep for the simple reason that June bought our milk at the market (we never used much, anyway) and I bought a paper, on the odd days when I was inclined to read one, from the rack beside the station. Now the grass is my *Journal*, and whispers news and gossip with green tongues that sometimes tell more than they know, or understand.

But enough of them and their small indiscretions—I vanished. Have you ever felt what it is to vanish? Do you know how a light feels when it goes out? Where the minutes disappear to when they pass? Let me tell you. . . .

I had finished writing that sentence about Africa, and made the period with a little stab of my pencil, and was just wondering if Madagascar and Africa were the right example, after all, when the pencil fell through my fingers to the paper, and rolling along the top of my desk, came to rest against the metal box in which I keep my stamps. It was not that the pencil had become too heavy for me to hold, but that my fingers had grown too light to hold it. I am tempted by the rooted courses of our language to say that I had the feeling then that the room around me, tole box, pencil, the brass inkstand with its devil face, desk, chair, books, walls, my bronze bust of Hogarth, had become unreal as the angel faces seen in clouds. The truth is otherwise: What I felt was no feeling, but certainty. I knew that I had lived my life among the shadows of shadows, that I had worked for money as I might have labored for fernseed, and spent my gains for the watermarks on paper, paper in a picture, the picture in a book seen lying open in a projection from a lens about to crack in an empty room of a vacant house. I stood up then and tried to rub my eyes and found that I saw through my own hands, and that they possessed personalities of their own, so that it was as though I nuzzled two friends, the left quick and strong, the right weaker, withdrawn, and a little dull. I saw a man—myself, I might as well admit, now, that he was myself—leave the room, walking through the misty wall and up into the sky as though he were climbing a hill; he turned toward me my own face cruel as a shark's, then threw it at me. I ducked and ran, lost at once until I met a tall, self-contained personage who was a tree, though I did not realize it until I had been with him for sometime. I think he was Doctor Hopkins' tree, actually—the big shade tree behind his house.

Dr. Hopkins lives on the next street over, two houses down. His tree spoke to me of the winds, and the different kinds of rains they blow, and as I talked I saw that he too was fading, and with him the light. A woman with white-blazoned black hair came carrying a lantern; I asked her about my daughter June.

I asked about June: that is true, but you cannot conceive how I feel when I write that, the pride that I did not gibber with fear to her (though to tell the truth I was very near it), the irony. She said, "Old man, what are you doing here?" and held her lantern up, and I understood—I will say "saw," though that is not the right word—that the lantern had come trailing this woman as a car might drag behind it a child's toy on a string. I said, "Am I among the nin?"

"Don't be a fool. What do you think names like that mean now?" She started to leave, and I followed her. We were not walking across a dark plain in a cold wind, but the mind is so accustomed to casting every event into images of this sort that it seemed so—except when I took particular note of what we were really doing, which was something like falling down a horizontal hole, a hole lined everywhere with roots and worms and strangely shaped stones, things all alive but ignoring us. "June!"the lantern said, and its woman looked at me. I thought at first that she was mocking me , then I understood that she was calling June, my poor daughter, for me, and that she was looking for her inside me, just as you might tell a man who says he cannot find his glasses that they might be in his pocket. I bent over to see, and kept on going, entering my body somewhere between my navel and my crotch.

I was walking into the withdrawal center again. Not withdrawal from drugs, which is what those places used to be when I was younger, but the place people—only young people, supposedly, people under thirty—withdrew from life itself. An operation had removed, at least for a time, certain wrinkles from my face; my beard was dyed, and young hair the shade of wheat had been sown in my scalp. They questioned me at the center, but only briefly—it is a way of disposing of the crowds, they say; a way to end crowding that involves no deaths. We shut our eyes to the sky and the sea in the seventies—now in the nineties we open doors to a darker, nearer empire than either, the place that is between stones that touch, that has lived for fifty thousand years in the black guts of caves, for six thousand in the empty rooms of old houses; and one of the doors is the door in this wall of bricks.

"Yes, what can we do for you?"

"I want to go."

"Yes," he said again. He waved me to a chair. "Tonight? Now?"

"Yes."

"My advice is to give yourself a cooling-off period. You don't have to, but that's what I'd advise you to do."

I shook my head.

"I don't mean a long time—just a couple of days."

"No."

He sighed. He was a young man, but the clipped mustache he wore made him look faintly old-fashioned, a little prissy. He said, "I'm going myself, you know. I wouldn't work here if I weren't. I wouldn't feel right about it."

"If you're going to go, why don't you go now?"

"My friend—I'm supposed to ask you questions, you don't ask me, understand. You want to go, and I think that's great, but if I say you can't, you can't. At least, not from here."

"How long are all these questions going to take?"

"I just wanted to explain. You know, when a person goes he doesn't go right away, at least not usually. He bounces."

I said, "I've seen them."

"Sure, everbody has. It's like this." He reached into a drawer of his desk and drew out a resilient ball cast of some clear elastometer shot with flakes of gold. He laid it on the desk top, and it began rolling very slowly toward the edge. "See, Mr. Ball doesn't like it up on the top of my desk; it's plastic up there, cold and narrow. He wants to go down to the floor—the wider world, you know? We give him a little push and down he goes. Watch what happens.''

The ball reached the edge and solemnly tumbled off, struck the floor and rose again until it was nearly as high as the top of the desk, dropped, rose, dropped, and rose. Each time it fell it made a soft patting, and this was the only sound in the silent building. ''Every time it bounces nearly as high as it was before, but not quite. Sooner or later it will stop bouncing and just roll around the floor—then it will be happy.''

''But meanwhile it's not?''

''It's not at peace. It's—you know—agitated. People are like that, and the older they are the more agitated they get; we won't take anybody over thirty, and you must be pretty close to that.''

''I'm twenty-nine.''

''Sure. Listen, the truth is that we do take them over thirty, but we don't advertise it because we're not supposed to. I mean, a woman comes in, she's fifty, and she's got cancer. I'm supposed to tell her no deal because she'd bounce too long.'' The young man shrugged fluidly, an Italianate shrug though his mustache was no darker than a fox's back. ''We take her and tell her to bounce where she won't be seen. You're thirty-five if you're a day.''

''I'm twenty-nine.''

''All right. Anyway, I try and *explain* to these people. It's hard on them, the bouncing in and out of nature. The N.I.N. is what they call them when they're gone, you know—the not in nature. But what about when they're on the shuttle between the worlds? And you're going to be there a long time. It's not like you were a child of sixteen or seventeen.''

''What interests me,'' I said, ''is that you seem to be implying that the nin exist at a lower energy level than we do.''

''Hell, it's a bit more complicated than that,'' the young man said, ''but have I talked you out of it?''

They gave me drugs both orally and intravenously; and made me lie down among humming, flashing machinery with wires on my head and feet and hands; and played music of a kind I had never heard before, while I read from a battered card. How much of what was done was done only to compel belief I do not know—perhaps it all was. *Never again, to walk as men walk, nevermore to die or sigh or cry. . . .* When it was over I stood up and the young man and a young woman shook my hand very solemnly and I thought that it would have been much more impressive if they had been dressed as doctor and nurse, but I did not tell them. When I was coming up my own front walk, the key in my hand, the whole world began to rise, pivoting (I think) on Madagascar so that I fell off the surface and was caught for a moment in the green arms of a neighbor's tree, and then, falling through them like rain, but upward, tumbled sidewise into the sky.

"Did you find her?" the lantern asked. I said that I had found her now, and indeed I saw her over the woman's shoulder, led by a tall, swaggering being of scarlet and gold. I ran to her and hugged her, and when I saw that the woman of the lamp had followed me I hugged her, too. "Be careful of Thag," she said. "You're going—we're—"

And then we three—but not the man in scarlet and gold—were standing beside the furnace in the basement of my own house. But June (until she vanished last night from her own locked room, while the dark-haired woman with the white forelock, who no longer is held aloft by her lantern, slept with me in the bed that has not held two since May died) would only cry, and tell us that her father the king would allow no one to mock her, and scream for fear the old man in the picture above our mantle would imprison her in the Piombi with Casanova. The dark-haired woman, whose eyes are blue and whose name is Laurel, said: "She has broken; we all break to some extent, and you have brought the wrong fragment."

Edgar Pangborn

THE LEGEND OF HOMBAS

HOMBAS was wiser than his people, but not stronger than Death, who makes no exceptions. Several times, even before the departure of the Spring Caravan, when the day's-end prayers had been spoken and he sat at the fringe of the night-fire in the compound, Hombas had seen the red bear Death approaching through the flames.

Hombas had also seen Death in the woods by daylight, the presence so like a true red bear that it would have deceived anyone else. He knew the truth, being Shaman and Chief Elder of the Commun. He had observed the red shadow, the Un-answerable, the Well-Intentioned, following one or another of the people. Unaware, the objects of Death's study continued their evening tasks, preparing the Commun to survive the night—stacking wood for the fires, making a circuit of the stockade, rounding up and counting the goats and children.

Trailing older members of the Commun (or the children, the timid weaker ones) and snuffling at their heels, the red bear might lift a black nose to savor the air for the scent of mortality. And now and then Death stood in front of them, obliging them to walk unknowingly through what only Hombas saw, the core of the mystery.

Hombas knew that Death had so far reached no decision.

Many times the red bear Death had risen to overwhelming shaggy height, twice the height of a man, and stared at Hombas

140

himself across the village street, small red eyes noncommittal like a pig's and sorrowfully wise like a man's. And now and then, when Hombas had been fasting or smoking the marawan pipe to invite wisdom, the red bear Death had drawn very close to observe him, vast russet head swaying back and forth barely an arm's length away. The last time this happened Hombas had said, quietly so as not to excite the small fry who enjoyed their evening romps around his hut: "I will go and wait for you in the open place when I must, but I am not ready." Death made no response to this, and he spoke again: "Or, if it will not offend you, I should like to wait until the return of the Spring Caravan, which must be soon (Jesus willing), so that I may bless the young men and hear for the last time what they tell of the out-world."

The red bear sighed hugely and went away, but only two nights later returned, standing close over Hombas, rising up on mighty hinder legs and gazing down, blotting away the night and the fire, and youth and age and time, the village and the world. The Spring Caravan was now shockingly overdue. Fear of disaster was chilling everyone. Hombas prayed once more to the red bear: "I ask you to allow me to remain until after the Ottoba harvest, for my people have always needed me when they were frightened."

At this appeal—Hombas hoped he had avoided loss of dignity in making it—the red bear Death showed neither anger nor assent, but shambled off to lie in the grass of the outground, under Hombas' eyes, until the stockade gate was closed for the night. Head on great flat paws, Death dozed, or looked toward the south when the children squealed or the little blattering goats walked through the presence.

Death lives in the south when at rest. The warm wind-spirits flee; that is why the south wind is hurried and soft like the touch of memory.

Hombas' people were wealthy, owning two other commum sites and prepared to defend them. It was nearly time, even in the usual order of affairs, for the people to move to the next of these locations—Flint Hill—after the necessary sacrifices and housecleaning. The people should never remain too long in one place. The ground sickens; squash, yam, and beans come to a puny harvest; the goats give poor milk. Men also sicken of sameness, just as they dread too big a change; then the gods are offended. Hombas saw in the eyes of his people that the move ought to be made soon, and all except the children would guess that on this occasion Hombas was not to travel with them. But he had not yet spoken, and one does not hurry the Chief of Elders.

They possessed other wealth, including a treasure of Old-Time coins for trading with the mad foreign city of Malone (some say Mayone), a four days' march toward the sunrise side of the world. In the spring, loaded with a winter's take of furs, or after the Ottoba harvest with handsome stacks of new-woven baskets, wood carvings, bows, necklaces of painted clay, doll toys of soft pine or plaited straw for children, the young men of the Caravan would gather for the good-luck prayers and Hombas' blessing. Then some skylarking, brag, and horse-play—boys are like that, and young men may now and then be allowed to act like boys—and in good time the Caravan would sort itself out and march in excellent silence down the dense green trail.

Those foolish people of Malone have no notion of commercial values. For a stack of fewer baskets than the fingers of one hand, they may pay a whole nickel coin, or even a penny. Apparently they don't know how grand a polish these red-brown things will take, nor how easily you can pound a hole in one of them with a steel point, and thus wear it for protection against smallpox and the malare. A soft people, the Maloners, and often you see grown mues among them behind their great stone walls, a great evil certain to bring a greater evil upon them, if they really don't understand the necessity of destroying these dreadful beings at birth. But their weapons and magic make them terrible. (Someday, says another Shaman who has grown old since Hombas' time, Malone shall fall desolate, and we shall go there to take what we will, and be rich forever.)

In a good year the Caravan would return with whole handfuls

of gorgeous coins—steel knives too, brass arrowheads nearly as good as steel, perhaps smoked fish, and soft cotton or wool cloth for the women's delight. It was a day for carnival and rejoicing when the Spring Caravan returned.

But where were they?

Hombas could remember the time, before his initiation, when the Elders had taken him aside and taught him how to measure the years of his life by spreading the fingers of both hands. You can measure days in the same fashion. He recalled how, after the circumcision and knocking out of an eye tooth and other agonies of passage, there came a year when his age was told by both hands together and one more hand. Thus on and on, adding a finger with every return of the moon of spring, until the joy was gone from it, and such counting became a reminder of stiffening in the joints, fading of sight, waning of all powers. He remembered the spring moon of nine fives, long ago, when he became a Shaman, and with the following winter moon an Elder. His age now was hardly to be credited: he numbered it by opening both hands together six times and then showing two fingers. Few but the gods can live to such an age. The people believe that when a Chief of Elders journeys over the waters marking the boundaries of life he becomes a god, and joins the divine Council of Elders in the country beyond the mountain Marsia.

The hands of Hombas counted far too many days since the Spring Caravan had gone. The red bear was walking in the firelight.

The red bear comes for all, but only the wise can observe the presence; only the wise remember that the red bear Death will take from them even wisdom. That is why we should listen to the wise, but not too much.

The Spring Caravan never returned. One young man at last crawled naked up the trail, gasping and torn. His right leg was broken; flies clung to gaping and festering wounds; he could not number the days he had spent in hobbling and creeping home. Once, driven off the trail by the smell of black wolf, he had lost his direction, and found it again, he said, only by the mercy of

Jesus, Shaman of Shamans. He was brought to Hombas, and in the dust before the blanket where Hombas sat he collapsed, digging clawed fingers into the dirt and beating his forehead on the ground, broken with shame that he should be the carrier of such news. But Hombas was gentle in speech, saying only: "You may tell us now, Absolon, son of Josson."

The young man told how the Spring Caravan, returning with rich goods from the trading at Malone, had been ambushed not far outside the walls of the city. Of the seven young men, only Absolon had survived. Him the ravagers had left for dead under the pile of other bodies, after stripping them of every smallest thing, every rag, bead, coin, ornament—even the wild parrot's feather that Absolon wore in his hair because the White Parrot was his patron.

The enemy were Sallorens, Absolon was sure, from the Ontara coast country, squat black-haired men who took no scalps. The savages of Eri in the southwest, or the red-haired Cayugas, would certainly have taken scalps and probably living captives, too, for the entertainment of their villages. These Sallorens, or anyway dark men tattooed just like them, are often seen at Malone, Absolon declared, wearing Mohan clothes and acting in other ways like Maloners. Then Absolon lifted his torn head and cursed Malone in all its days and years, for he believed there had been a conspiracy, Malone sending word to the Sallorens of the Caravan's coming.

"Do you know this, Absolon? Perhaps they were lying in wait for any caravan that might appear."

"It may be," said Absolon. "Before the Chief Elder's wisdom I am a fool and a nothing."

The women wailed and scored their breasts; they pulled out their hair and raved. The other young men who had not been chosen to go with the Caravan smeared their faces with dung, and wept, and sharpened their knives. Then all became still, for after Absolon had been taken away to be cared for and if possible healed, Hombas called a Council of the other four Elders. When the old men discuss what is to be done, there should be no speech or foolish noise.

The Elders grouped by the night-fire. Hombas said: "My

brothers and my children, this calamity was foretold. But I, Hombas, Chief of Elders, failed to read the signs truly. I am in sorrow. For many days and nights I have seen the red bear."

Isaia, second in age and virtue of the Elders, asked: "The red bear, the Well-Intentioned, has not chosen, Chief of Elders?

"He has not chosen."

The Elder Isaia said: "The Chief of Elders is burdened with years and long service to Jesus, Shaman of Shamans."

And others: "Jesus, Shaman of Shamans, knows what is to be."

"The people shall move to Flint Hill," Hombas told them, "as soon as the bodies of the young men have been recovered, if that may be. They shall be given as heroes to the burning. After this, Jero, and Adam, and the Elder Elahu, shall go to Flint Hill and see that the stockade is in repair, the ground fit, the dwellings clean and sound, the wood gathered, and the night-fire restored."

"It shall be done as the Chief of Elders explains."

"I, Hombas, shall not go to Flint Hill."

"The saying of the Chief of Elders is hard."

"I have lived six tens and two."

"Make us to understand the will of the Spirit."

"I foretold a safe journey for the Caravan. Now the young men who went with my blessing are dead, my head is covered with ashes, the women tear their breasts."

Isaia said again, as was proper, but with the noise a voice makes when ambition mixes uneasily with kindness: "The Chief of Elders is heavy with years and godlike in long service."

"Before the sun rises ten men shall go and recover the bodies of young men, if that may be, if the forest has not taken them. But now the people must understand a hard thing: Without these men we have not the strength to carry war against the Sallorens this year. After the winter moons perhaps it may be done, under the guidance of another Chief of Elders, when I have journeyed over the waters that mark the boundaries of life."

"Amen, amen."

"At your departure for Flint Hill, I shall go out to the open place and await the Unanswerable. Let none look back.''

''Amen, O Hombas, Chief of Elders.''

''And now, O Lord of Hosts,'' said Hombas, ''deliver us from evils and evildoing, in the name of the Father, the Son, and the Spirit! May the wombs of our women bear, may the earth bring forth, and the white-scut deer be plentiful. And may my children and my brothers dwell with one another in justice and mercy, amen.''

''Amen.''

After quiet, the Elder Dorson said: ''Hombas, Chief of Elders, the fourth child of the woman of Jero turns blue in the face and scarcely breathes. The child is, to be sure, a girl.''

''I will carry her with me to the open place, in Jesus' name.''

And the Elder Magann: ''Hombas, Chief of Elders, an earthen pot in the house of Adam cracked last night for no clear reason as it stood by the fire.''

''Let it be broken in small shards, for exorcism. The fragments may be left with me in the open place.''

The Elder Isaia said with respect: ''Hombas, Chief of Elders, I have a sleek male kid not yet weaned of its mother.''

''This I accept as first offering to the Unanswerable. Let it be tethered in the open place at the time of your departure. Should the people ratify you, dear and well-spoken Isaia, as Chief of Elders, may you live long and continue to love justice.''

Then Hombas, who had lived for many years without women, entered his hut and laid across his eyes the white cloth that brings prophetic dreams. In the village, no loud talk, no more wailing, out of respect for the rest and sleep of him who had been Chief of Elders and who would not go with the people on their next journey.

And Hombas dreamed of his own journey to come, over the waters that mark the boundaries of life.

He stood on the bank in his dream, while the Ferryman approached through fog like one reluctant. By the mystery of dreaming, Hombas was able to observe his face—calm it was, devoid of anger and joy—as he could not observe the face of a companion who stood beside him in the heaving vapor. It was proposed to Hombas by this companion that he might not be ready for the passage. To him Hombas replied: "I am ready in years, ready in weariness; my joints pain me, my memory mocks me like a naughty servant. In other ways, can one ever be ready, my companion? Is not life too sweet to abandon even when the stream widens and moves sluggishly with a burden of memories? What more must I do before I rest with my fathers?"

The reply of his companion was not in words, but Hombas understood that some further labor might indeed remain—but it would be for him to discover the nature of it. And as though he had come to Hombas for no purpose except to offer a troubling communication, the faceless companion was now gone—all along he might have been no more than a heavy part of the mist. In his place the red bear stood half-seen, surely too vast to accompany Hombas in the little boat, but ready perhaps to swim in the black water beside him, or to drift through the obscurity as a phantom. As one who had loved and served his fellows a long time, Hombas understood how the most immense and inescapable of forces may well appear unreal to human beings—they always have—until these forces sweep them away: flood, fire, war, pestilence, human folly, or that death which is merely the end of living.

The Ferryman was poling an oarless boat. This might mean that the waters marking the boundaries of life are as shallow as they are slow. It was an instructive, amusing detail that he could have told the village children who liked to tumble and chase each other around his hut, climb his legs, sprawl in his lap and fall asleep, tease for some little present or a kiss—children are not repelled by the truly wise, only by the half-wise. But the red bear stirred and sighed, and Hombas remembered it was not fitting for him to think of seeing the children again, nor the village, nor any of the faces of his own kind.

The Ferryman grounded his boat on the gravel margin. Hombas offered him the coin of passage. But the gaunt naked fellow said: "This is only metal. From Hombas, Chief of Elders, more is expected."

"What must I pay then?" asked Hombas. "The wise are poor

in the world, Ferryman; their chief reward is not much more than uneasy tolerance."

"Will you pay me your hopes?"

"If I have my hopes no longer, can I rest among my fathers? I see that perhaps I might, and—yes, rather than stay here on this bank among these homeless vapors, I will pay you my hopes."

"It is offered grudgingly. It is not enough. Will you pay me your visions and your memories of human love?"

"Without them, Ferryman, how shall I be better than this broken rock and sand, which has no will except the water's will?"

"You are not ready for passage," said the Ferryman. "Go back in the world a little while, Hombas, in your tattered loincloth and nakedness and pride. Go back and labor again, if it is only the labor of learning humility."

And Hombas woke, putting away the cloth from his eyes and seeing the tranquil night-fire outside his hut. He heard muted voices with other village sounds, the desolate laughter of a loon in the marsh, a night-hawk, a wolf's howl from the midnight hills. Up in the maple leaves a wind was rippling in the current of spring. The dream disturbed him in his heart. Before first light—he knew the ten men were about to go and recover the bodies of the slain, if that might be—a boy came softly to tell him the messenger Absolon had died in the night, of fever and the festering of his wounds.

Hombas wished he might consult a wiser head as to the meaning of all that was happening, but he knew, as sober truth, that however imperfect his wisdom, no one wiser than himself was in the village or perhaps anywhere in the world; unless it might be the children, who have no time to transmit the virtue of their simplicity before it is gone—that is why we should listen to children.

The bodies of the young men were brought back, what the Sallorens and the forest scavengers had left of them, and were given as heroes to the burning. All that day Hombas sat on his blanket in the compound fasting, his eyes in pain from the smoke of the pyre. It hung sullen over the village in the windless

ours. He was aloof, as was proper for one lately Chief of
Elders, unapproachable and old. He thought of the young men,
prayed for them. He thought too of the older days, of the years
outside his experience but spoken of by his father, who had
known himself to be a great-grandson of the West Wind. When
at last the funeral songs were done and the blaze not more than
heat remembered, evening was coming on again, while in the
village certain quiet preparations were being made for departure
in the morning.

It was not fitting that Hombas should pay heed to these. He
meditated through another night on his dream of that shallow
river marking the boundaries of life, of the Ferryman's hard
sayings. He did not see the red bear.

At dawn the younger wife of Isaia brought him goat's milk,
and the kid that was to be tethered near him in the open place. As
he drank the milk and blessed her, the Elder Isaia came also to
kneel before him, and said: "Hombas, venerable Shaman, the
Elders have chosen me to hold the office that you honored, in
Jesus' name. I pray you bless me to this service, Hombas."

They say that Hombas smiled as he blessed Isaia, who was
not a cheerful man, and placed on him the sacred deer-bone
necklace that confers courage and quickness of mind. They say
also that Isaia, in his time as Chief of Elders, governed well,
though sometimes hesitant and anxious, and that the precedents
upholding his decisions were very often the judgments of
Hombas. "Be content, Isaia," Hombas said. "It is a brave
journey between midnights." This has been remembered,
though few agree on all that Hombas meant by it.

Then there came to him the aging warrior Jero; he had taken
from his woman the infant girl five days old whose face turned
blue and who could not breathe except with difficulty, bringing
her to Hombas; behind him his woman watched dry-eyed, and
did not speak. The baby, as Hombas received her in his arms,
curled a fist around his finger and for awhile her gasping breath
came more quietly. The people remember this, not as a miracle
but as a certain evidence of divine grace. And when Hombas
rose, holding her in the hollow of his arm and leading the
unweaned kid with his left hand, it was seen that the kid

followed him without any tugging at the leash of leather, and that the child had fallen asleep. Hombas said then to the woman of Jero: "Be content, Rashel, with what no power can change. If she is not to know joy in living, neither can she know sorrow."

Hombas went out beyond the stockade of the village, through the pasture where the goats were being herded together for the journey to Flint Hill, and up a winding path in the long grass, among juniper and scattered boulders and tangles of wild raspberry canes, to the open place, a wide area where flat granite covered a shoulder of the hillside; at the western end of the outcropping of rock grew a thick spruce that held away the wind. Near this tree the good man Adam had brought the shards of his broken pot, and a sound jar filled with spring-water. Hombas blessed him, and sat here with the still sleeping child, gazing over undulant hills in the south, and toward the mountain Marsia in the southwest, distant under the sky of spring.

The little goat he had tethered somewhat below the open place out of his sight. It was necessary that it should bleat and call, being a first offering to the powers who would come for Hombas himself when the time was right. The small creature might feel desolate and abandoned for a time, until the gods of the forest came and released it; but they would do so. It would not be fitting for Hombas to witness their coming. The forest gods ought not to be drawn by trickery, or against their will, into human observation. They are lonely ones. That is why the bats, who are the gods of those night-thoughts that flutter past too quickly to be questioned, never appear by day. Or if one does, a good man will help it to a tree-hollow where it can wait on the return of dark.

Holding the infant, Hombas meditated on death, and found it strange that all he could remember of his people's thought on the matter, including his own, had been concerned not with the thing itself but with hope or legend or speculation concerning some life beyond the incident of death: as though death were no more than a passage, an opening in the woods. *But what if it is not so? What if death is no passage at all, only the termination of thought, feeling, presence? Who has seen the soul that is to board the Ferryman's little boat and cross the waters that mark the boundaries of life? If none has seen it, can a wise man accept a belief in the existence of it?*

Was it my soul far wandering that spoke with the Ferryman, and with someone faceless, in my dream? All people dream, and most dreams are ridiculous. In sleep are we perhaps not wandering away from the body into the country of the spirits as the wise men of the past have taught us, but merely lying still and thinking fantastically in our sleep? . . . Now this might mean that there is no soul, and even that the wise men of the past were not quite wise.

The morning drew on with quiet, in springtime coolness. Hombas sensed that the people had gone, and his mind traveled a little way with them on the obscure trail to Flint Hill, and let them go, returning to the open place. The child did not wake; her breathing was very shallow, her pallor more waxen than bluish, with pinched tiny nostrils. Now and then Hombas waved away a hovering fly. It might have been more fitting, more pleasing to the forest gods, to set her out now on the rock or where the kid was tethered, but Hombas preferred to hold her fading warmth against his own until her small, foredoomed struggle for continuing life should end. It would not be long.

He meditated on the tales and fancies and histories of the Old Time, the Age of Sorcerers. It was darkly long ago—five generations, even two fives, who can say? Hombas' father when he was young had met a very old man in Malone who said that as a boy he had seen one of the Old-Time death-sticks of heavy metal, in possession of an ancient redheaded Cayuga. That savage had told him how there used to be pellets made by the Sorcerers, each containing a devil, which could be placed inside the hollow stick. Then, by command of the stick's owner, the devil would burst forth at the other end with such frightful power that anything in its path was instantly killed. Catrishes, those pellets were called. The Cayuga assured the boy they had all been used up and swept out of existence in Old-Time—at least, he said, looking sly, he *thought* they had. He broke open the stick at the large end so that the boy might look through the hollow passage inside and see the strange regular spirals cut into the metal, and then made him jump out of his skin by slamming a foot on the ground and shouting "*Brroom!*" Cayugas never have any manners. The boy, telling the story as an old man, was said to have said that the Maloners who saw the stick had no belief in the powers of it. They claimed it was just a hollow iron bar with wooden fittings, part of one of the Sorcerers' miraculous machines; or perhaps the Sorcerers had used it to beat their servant devils and make them obey.

Hombas knew other tales. In the Age of Sorcerers, myriads of magicians rushed about all over the earth in wheeled carts that moved of themselves by a horrid magic. Hombas himself, when young, hunting with two companions and following a wounded woods buffalo too far to the south, dangerously close to Cayuga country, had come upon one of the enormous roads built by the Sorcerers to serve these hell-carts. Straight as a spear the road ran and level as a stream, cutting a valley from hilltop to hilltop with mighty disdain for any lesser rises or hollows. Vines had been able to cross it here and there, especially the poison ivy and jinna-creeper, with their countless busy rootlets. Elsewhere the road stretched bleak and clear, pitted with cracks and holes but nearly lifeless, a track of desolation through the green. Seeing this thing, one could understand how the curse of the good Jesus had fallen on the Sorcerers and destroyed them and all their works.

Hombas and his friends had known better than to venture out on that horror. Yet, the young men do say that the Townfolk make some use of these roads, near Malone and those other places where they have their clustered dwellings, and impregnable high walls to hold off brown tiger and black wolf and red bear. The feet of their horses and oxen cannot endure the surface of the ancient roads, of course, but the Maloners and their kind, with leather shoes and an unlimited store of foolishness, walk out on them and apparently take no harm.

The Sorcerers rode in the machines that climbed through the air beyond human vision. They could make the air vibrate, too, and so talk magically with each other across many miles. And they traveled back and forth at will between the earth and the moon.

The moon is a globe that the god Jehova set spinning many centuries ago along with the sun, in such a way that the two run a strictly ordered course above the earth and below the earth. The heat of the sun is life and day; the light of the moon is wisdom and night. A long time from now, the force of the god's original cast will run down (according to his own foresight) and then both sun and moon will fall into the sea that runs all around the field of the earth. In that time will be only starlight; there will be no day. The earth will stand without heat or wisdom. The people, all of them, will have crossed the waters that mark the boundaries of life.

In the time of the Sorcerers the moon was larger in the skies, and often red. And the impious traveling of the Sorcerers to the moon resulted in the first of their great punishments. The moon-people came out of the center of their globe and made war on them. The Sorcerers fought hard, but the moon-people, whom Jesus loves also, defeated them with a mightier science (that is an Old-Time word for magic), destroying countless numbers of the Sorcerers' flying craft. Before the Sorcerers' armies on the moon were annihilated by the moon-people, the colossal warfare had laid waste enormous areas of that globe and created mountainous ruins.

There is never any profit in trying to tell of these things to the Maloners. They build walls, contrary to Jesus' commands, and they cherish the ugly fancy that the earth itself is a globe, and there is no truth in them. When they die, the Ferryman cannot take them because they do not believe in the god Jehova nor in Jesus his prophet, but follow the false prophet Abraham. At death their poor homeless spirits go wandering, swept here and there until they become caught in the tree branches. When the wind strikes those branches in the barren time of winter, you hear them crying.

This is how you may know the truth of what happened to the Sorcerers on the moon. When the moon is full, look on those gray marks that seem like shadows. Those are blighted areas left by the war up there, just like the desert of Eri and other places that the Sorcerers left ruined on the earth before they perished.

The child made a noise too small and fleeting for a groan. Her breathing ceased. Hombas recited the prayer for those dying in infancy, that the Ferryman should let them pass without payment of a coin. Rising stiffly with her, he felt the spring chill with sudden acuteness; his joints ached. Dizziness from the hours of fasting laid hold of him, and he staggered.

These disorders could be overcome. Presently he was able to carry the baby's lifeless body to the far edge of the rocks. There the Forest People would find her, or the Well-meaning Winged Ones whose faces are not to be looked on because the god Jehova for his own reasons has made them horrible.

He had set down the little corpse and made the sign of the cross over her, when from no great distance an intolerable cry of outrage and pain rang and rang through the woods, echoing metallically from bare tree-trunks and rock surfaces. Shrill it was, keening and prolonged, coming from some great chest of powerful resonance. Black wolf could not have made that noise. Red bear does not speak, except to growl or chuckle or snort a little: The red bear expects deference from everyone, except the Maloners who are foolish and sinful, and has no need of threatening or angry cries. Hombas stood paralyzed with wonder, shrinking too, for it was a sound to make the flesh cringe regardless of courage. He trembled in the certainty that he would again hear the anguished voice. He did, once more, and the sound trailed off in a long groan. Brown tiger never sent forth that roar of agony. If this were a victim of brown tiger—woods buffalo, maybe, or elk—it would have had no chance for a second cry. And what grass-eater could utter such vast rage?

There came distant thrashing noises, and a muffled pounding as if a giant's fist were hammering the earth. Then Hombas belatedly remembered that not very long ago, before the departure of the Spring Caravan, the people had built a deep deadfall near the Open Place, where they had found a trail beaten by those vermin, the wild pigs, attackers of children and raiders of the gardens. Hombas had approved the digging at the time. Presumably the swine had proved too clever to be deceived, and so he had heard no more said about it. All the same Hombas found it shocking that he could have forgotten it.

High time indeed to go and sit in the Open Place.

Well—wild boar never made such a noise as that. And Hombas reflected: *In the forest live many gods we do not know. Perhaps one of them has need of me. Perhaps Jesus, Shaman of Shamans, has offered me opportunity to do some service before I cross the waters that mark the boundaries of life.*

Somewhat lightheaded but no longer much afraid, he glanced toward the sun, astonished to note how far the day had advanced beyond noon. He let himself down from the rock, moving more easily as his muscles limbered with the action, and moved off under the trees in the direction of that pounding. He heard now a heartrending moaning, muffled, high, nasal, broken now and then by a snap of jaws. So it might be bear after all, for they chatter their teeth like that in anger; but surely not a red bear. In Hombas' memory, no red bear had ever been caught in a trap or deadfall.

Hombas' foot caused a dry branch to crack under him; the moaning and pounding ceased. The noise had summoned him; now the being, whoever it was, knew he was coming, and so fell silent. Hombas was sure of the direction. He called politely: "I who come to you am Hombas who was Chief of Elders. If you are a god, you may command me, a believer in the laws. If you are a forest thing, I come in mercy."

He heard no reply. But the Forest People are not given to needless speech, except for the wind spirits, and what they say is more music than speaking. He hobbled on therefore, no longer trying to move with quiet. He found the trail that had been tramped, not recently, by the wild swine. The smell in his nostrils was the feral, fishy scent of bear. He came to the edge of the pit, where the branches hiding the deadfall had been broken in. Rearing a tormented head above the surface of the ground was the red bear Death, who was blind.

With the eyes of the flesh Hombas saw him, an old and mighty male who had evidently been blind in his right eye for a long time, since the socket was shrunken and fallen in—perhaps an arrow wound, or a slash in some battle with his own kind. Now the other eye was squeezed shut, leaking tears, and in the fur of the great, round, innocent face were tangled the bodies of many wild bees, smashed by the bear's paw—but one of them must have carried a sting to the eyeball. The bear's head was turned toward Hombas, but only because he had heard the approach. When Hombas stepped silently to one side, the creature did not move in response to the action.

With the senses of his flesh Hombas heard, some distance up the trail, the still furious snarling hum of the hive. The bee warriors had not pursued the ravisher this far, or perhaps had lost sight of him when he fell into the pit in his pain and blindness.

Hombas smelled the bear's blood. In falling he had pierced a hind foot on one of the sharpened stakes in the pit. He had torn the foot free, but other stakes prevented him from winning a purchase with his hind claws on the dense clay walls. He had pounded at the edges of the pit, without aim in his darkness, trying to break down a passage to freedom, but the clay was tight, the pit dug deep and wide by the people with good steel tools from Malone. Now the bear had ceased that effort.

Smelling and hearing man, he roared in despair and agony. He lunged toward Hombas, bringing down both forepaws tremendously on the edge. But then his blind head dropped between them, and he let it remain there, as if he prayed.

With the senses of the flesh, the knowledge of a hunter, the wisdom of a Shaman, Hombas observed and understood all this, and feared the tortured beast, and pitied him.

With the eyes of the spirit, Hombas knew that the red bear Death might be about to die.

Hombas asked him: "Has the god Jehova decreed that Death shall die? Is it possible?"

He won no answer. In the faintness from his age and long fasting, he believed the waters that mark the boundaries of life must be flowing not far from this lonely place in the woods, and without sight of him he felt the presence of the Ferryman. Poling the little boat (perhaps) nearer to this shore, expecting that Hombas might by now have discovered what labor it was he ought still to perform. *What will become of the Ferryman, if Death is about to die?*

Hombas moved away, disturbed by an inner rejoicing not altogether candid nor genuine. Death was to be no more—why, if so, all the Forest People should be singing, and every leaf should smile with an inner sunlight. But he, Hombas, was the only one who knew it yet—he alone among all the wise men. Soon all would know it. *No more dying! (But if flowers do not fade, how shall new flowers grow?)*

He walked feebly down the trail, unwilling to look back although the blind bear might be silently calling him. *I shall not die. I shall live forever. (With these aching joints, this weariness?—oh, even that way, is life not dear?) I shall enjoy the night-fire, the changes of life in the compound, the children, the meditation, the sharing of wisdom, the tenderness of returning spring. (But if flowers do not fade, how can there be rebirth, how can there be spring?)*

I must go to Flint Hill and tell my people. I return to you—hear me! There is to be no more dying. I, Hombas, Chief of Elders, have permitted Death to die although he prayed to me. I bring you life eternal—rejoice, rejoice! Your children shall not perish! Never shall your beloved die!

He found laughter, running down the trail, stumbling, weeping and shouting: "*Life eternal! Hear me, my people! Life eternal!*"

But in this clumsy ecstasy he tripped on a root, and saved himself by clutching at a branch, and stood there wavering, dizzy and gasping for breath. His eyes cleared. He stared along the branch. A fat greenish blowfly lit on it not far from his fingers; she was ripe with eggs and bloated with carrion meals, and he saw her accept the mounting and penetration of a male. The two squatted there linked in copulation, seeming to regard him. *No dying? . . .*

Hombas returned to the pit. He spoke a little to the red bear Death, but the legend does not say whether this was a true conversation or only the voiced reflections of a man with a difficult task to perform. He searched the region around the pit until he found where his people had cut an ash tree to use in making the deadfall. They had left the long butt on the ground, wanting only the flimsy upper branches. Moving this fourteen-foot log was surely a task for two men in their prime, yet Hombas accomplished it, levering it with small sticks we suppose, and resting often.

He worked it to the edge of the deadfall. He said to the blinded beast: "It is well that we met, who have need of each other." And then he slid the log down so that an end rested against one of the stakes, a bridge on an easy slant for the bear's escape. And he sat by the trail waiting.

That is how Death became blind. But the people who know the legend call Hombas blessed, because of his mercy to us.

Gail Kimberly

THE FIRE FOUNTAIN

IN a city of glass and steel, on a minutely symmetrical street, in a geometrically perfect building that housed relics of the past in orderly rows, the four friends were together. They were on the fifteenth floor, in the "Ancient Modes of Travel" exhibit, strolling past bulky, four-wheeled vehicles that had been powered by fossil fuel; awkward, wasp-shaped fliers with propellors on their roofs, and smooth-hulled seacraft.

The four friends were Bramfel, Orin, Greely, and Anatol—all much alike in build and appearance, since they had been made from the same pattern—and all were robots, but different in personality, and of different age and experience. Orin, the oldest, had passed all but six months of his allotted two-hundred-year lifespan. Greely and Anatol were half his age. Bramfel was the youngest, a mere forty-eight.

They passed along the line of vehicles that were each on a plastic platform, spotlighted, labeled, and catalogued, and did not know they were looking at their own close relatives, for the vehicles and the robots had both been the brainchildren of man. But the robot race now denied that man had ever existed. Whatever records human beings might have left before they died out, nearly eight centuries ago, had either been obliterated, forgotten, or went unrecognized. Man was considered a myth, a superstition. The robots believed these artifacts before them had been devised by other robots like themselves—more primitive in design and more limited in intellect, to be sure, but still ancestors of their own kind.

And so they wondered at the clumsy construction of machines that had flown robots through the skies before the time they could fly under their own power; and machines that had driven them along the roads before the roads had become obsolete. They stopped before the boats.

This one, Bramfell told the others over his open telebeam. *A boat like this with sails, and a motor to use only when we have to. We can explore the sea and the islands, endure all kinds of weather, examine all manner of marine and terrestrial life. Think of the experiences we can store!*

A boat! Orin stroked the hull with his metal hand. *I've flown over the seas and swum in them, but never in all my years have I tried to sail over them in a vessel like this!*

Bramfel turned on his vocalizer and gave a brief command in the clicking speech the robots sometimes used. There was a sudden hum of power and the air around them turned to mist, and they were standing on the deck of a rolling sloop, riding deep blue waves, striped orange and green sails taut above them. The illusor gave them a sixty-second sample of what it would be like to be on this type of sailboat and then, with a whine, it turned off and they were once again standing on the solid floor before the model.

It will be dangerous, came the thought from Anatol.

But what a challenge! Greely seemed enthusiastic.

And that's what life is all about, Orin reminded them. *Experience . . . danger . . . knowledge to store in our data vaults and thus to mature and grow wise.*

The idea of a voyage on an ancient ship had come to Bramfel the first time he'd seen this model, and he was glad that his friends seemed to like it. It would take four of them to handle the ship. *We'll have one built exactly like this one, bigger, of course, and stocked with an emergency engine. Should we have our powers reduced to make it more of a challenge?*

They all considered this, and finally Greely answered. *We should have our anti-grav flight motors removed, at any rate, so we won't be tempted to fly out of danger.*

Really! Anatol objected. *The whole project sounds perilous enough as it is, without crippling ourselves, too.*

But he was overruled by the others, and the decision was made to leave as soon as the boat was ready.

They went out of the building, and while Greely and Anatol hurried away to keep appointments, Bramfel strolled with Orin through the museum's gardens.

Orin seemed troubled, but he had shut off his telebeam so that Bramfel had to wait until he was ready to communicate again. He admired the precisely patterned flower beds and the crystal fountains, and at last Orin opened his beam.

Bramfel, although you're young, you're a logical, sensible robot. I'm going to tell you something I wouldn't tell the others. They wouldn't understand, but I believe you will.

Bramfel, pleased at the compliment, urged him to go on.

I have lived many years and seen many strange things, Orin told him. *Now we are voyaging together on what will be my last adventure before my data vaults are audited for the last time and Central Agency decides if I have matured enough to be promoted to a high position, or if I will be sent back to the factory to have my memory erased and my body refitted and sent out again.*

You'll be promoted, Orin, I feel sure. You're very wise.

Perhaps you'll feel differently when I tell you this. Orin paused for a moment and then made the strangest statement Bramfel had ever heard. *I believe in the existence of man.*

Man! But that's irrational! The thought went out over his telebeam before he could stop it, but Orin had apparently been expecting this reaction. He seemed unperturbed.

Wait a moment, Bramfel, before you form any conclusions. Remember that I have lived nearly two hundred years, and have seen many strange things.

What? What have you seen?

I have seen footprints. Not the pawprints of animals, but the footprints of something that walked upright on feet that had no rubber treads and no vent holes on the bottom, as ours do.

Apes, Bramfel suggested.

In the forests of the north country? No. And where I have seen

*the footprints, I have found fires of wood and brush lying
deserted, still glowing when I found them. Apes do not make
fires. Bramfel, I have seen the ruins of ancient buildings,
imperfectly built yet sturdy. Not the works of robots.*

*But Orin, no one has ever seen a man. There have always
been tales about human beings, but surely someone would have
told about seeing them if they existed?*

*And risk being reported to Central Agency as irrational? No,
Bramfel, I think men have been seen by others, but no one has
dared risk bringing back stories about them.*

Bramfel considered this. Man—the most vicious, most
dangerous species in the world, if the stories about them were
true. But no, such tales couldn't be true! The universe was, after
all, logical, and all things existing in it were logical. Man was an
irrational, illogical, mythical being that could not exist. He was
said to be made of flesh, yet able to think and reason. No
creature of flesh could reason and think, as far as he knew. Not
only that, but man was susceptible to disease, death, and decay.
And man was said to kill. No logical being would take a life that
could not be replaced.

Orin went on. *I believe, Bramfel, that human beings know of
our existence and stay out of our way.*

Why? Why would they not want to meet us?

*I don't know. But they hide in remote corners of the world. I
believe that travelers that are missing every now and then have
been captured by men and perhaps destroyed. It is said humans
will render a robot inoperative and use his components for their
own dark purposes.*

Why are you telling me all this? Bramfel felt uncomfortable
receiving such information, especially from a robot he respected
as much as Orin.

*Because I want to find man on this voyage, and I want you to
help me. You'll be heading this expedition, and I want your
purpose to be the same as mine. Bramfel, when Central Agency
audits my data vaults, they're going to find out that I hold this
belief they consider irrational. What will be my chances for
promotion then? But if I can prove the belief is not irrational,
perhaps even bring back a specimen of man, or some irrefutable
evidence. . . .*

It would certainly be an interesting challenge, Bramfel knew, searching for a mythical being. But why not? After all, it would be Orin's last voyage, his last chance, and it meant so much to him. *Very well,* he told the old robot. *But shouldn't we tell the others, too?*

You know Anatol is too conventional to even consider the possibility of human beings existing. He'd refuse to go on such a trip. And Greely cares only for the experience, the excitement, and the danger. No, I don't want them to know until we have some concrete evidence to show them.

A fifty-six-foot yawl was built and stocked with an emergency engine, depthfinder, tools, and greases with which to repair themselves if needed, and assorted gear for the voyage. Then, to add to the danger and thus make the experience more valuable, they had their abilities deliberately reduced. Instead of being able to lift a ton, the strength in their arms was cut down to be sufficient for only one-tenth that much. Instead of being able to run as fast as the fastest animal and to fly under their own power, they could now only trot, earthbound. Their hearing, too, was cut down so that they could hear sounds only in their immediate vicinity.

Four safeguards were left them: their visual receptors, that could see by night and by day with equal ease; their thinking capacity had not been diminished; their components had been specially sealed to withstand the elements and the pressure of the sea depths, and air-lungs had been installed to make their metal bodies buoyant in the water. They could voyage for only six months, for their atomic batteries would need recharging at the end of that time, but in six months they could store a wealth of data.

And so the *Seahorse* and its crew sailed from Whitecliff Point and went north to the frigid waters near the North Pole, where the robots witnessed the splendor of the northern lights and the glitter of stars on the icebergs. Bramfel searched the bleak tundra with Orin, but found no trace of human beings.

Then they sailed southeast, exploring the rocky coasts where gannets nested, and the islands where gannets nested, and the

islands where deer and moose wandered. While Anatol and
Greely dived under the waves to observe life in the depths,
Bramfel and Orin searched forests and plains along the coast,
looking for man, but finding no sign of him. In temperate and
tropical climates they landed on islands with strange varieties of
animal life, but no evidence of any other inhabitants, until they
had been voyaging for more than five months and it was time to
return to civilization. Bramfel felt by now that Orin's stories had
not been the exact truth. Perhaps in his desire to justify his
belief, the old robot had misinterpreted things he had found
years ago. Perhaps time had distorted his memory. Orin didn't
seem to be discouraged, but explored each new place with the
same enthusiasm; still Bramfel was tiring and felt that in his
search for the legend he might be missing out on adventures that
would be more meaningful.

One warm, sunny day when the sea lay like sapphire glass
around them and there was no breeze to fill their sails, Bramfel
decided to dive underwater to see if he could catch a glimpse of a
giant squid that Greely claimed to have seen while swimming
underwater earlier that day. He asked Orin to go with him, and
together they sank down into the half-light of the undersea
world.

Curious fish followed them as they descended, until they had
passed the point where the sun's rays could reach and blackness
closed in around them, the only light the amber glow from their
visual receptors. Down, and still farther down they went, to the
depths where the squids lived. They swam among rocky reefs,
frightening schools of fish that were no more than tiny ovals of
pale light darting between them, searching for the giant squid. A
mass of seaweed gathered on Bramfel's leg and he had to stop to
untangle it, holding to a rock as he did so, but as the seaweed
came loose, he saw that it wasn't a rock he was clutching. It was
a metal tube, encrusted with corals that disguised its shape. He
summoned Orin over his telebeam. The old robot swam to him
in answer to his call, and together they pried away the organisms
clustered on the tube and studied it carefully. It was about ten
inches in diameter and probably made of steel, although the
metal was pitted and marred by age and the encroaching sea life.

When they swam back a short distance to get a better look, they saw that the tube was protruding from a huge metal structure that lay on the sea bottom, and there were other metal tubes sticking out from its side.

It's a ship! Orin was excited.

Bramfel went closer again, brushing away a swarm of curious fish that clustered around him. There seemed to be glass here, just above the first deck, partly visible under the crust of sea animals. He peeled these off a small area and uncovered a round pane of glass, pitted and corroded like the metal that held it. He pressed his face to the glass, his visual receptors beaming into the blackness, and looked through. The sea had taken over the inside of the ship, too, but he could see, after a time of studying, the remains of walls that had been formed a compartment, and the shapes of fixtures inside it. Fixtures he did not recognize.

No robot built this ship. Orin's face was beside his, pressed to the thick glass.

But then who else?

Human beings! I knew we'd find something!

Perhaps ancient robots. . . . Bramfel was reluctant to jump to conclusions.

There's no mention of this type of vessel in all recorded history. Why would robots need a ship with metal tubes along its sides? What about those fixtures? What would they be used for? And why would robots need a ship divided up into units the way this one is, as though its occupants needed to be separated from each other when they traveled? We don't have any such need.

Bramfel drew back from the glass, puzzled, trying to correlate this new data with information already in his vault. He swam over and studied the metal pipes again. He could not guess what purpose these might serve, either. When he looked up, Orin was nowhere to be seen.

Bramfel moved along the side of the ship to find out where he might have gone, and then Orin's call reached him. At the same time, he saw an opening in the ship, just beyond him. He swam in and there was Orin, rubbing his metal hand against part of a ruined wall.

What is it? Have you found something?

A metal plate set into this wall. It has markings on it. Orin traced his finger over the faint lines etched into the square plate.

Bramfel studied the writing that was not in any language he had ever seen, and as Orin's finger moved, he tried to decipher it. "S. S. *Albany.*" *What do you suppose it is? The name of this ship?*

Probably. Orin dug his fingers around the square edge of the plate and tried to pry it loose, and Bramfel pried at another corner. They were so engrossed in trying to free the plate that it was only when they were aware of varicolored lights glowing in the corner of their vision, and looked up to see a huge shape moving inside the ship, not far from them, that they remembered the squid.

Both of them headed immediately for the opening. When they had passed through it, Bramfel looked back to see the giant squid rocketing out of the aperture. Using a metal tube for leverage, he rose out of its path.

Panic gripped him now. The squid was huge, at least three times his size, and might do them serious damage if it attacked them. He saw that Orin was swimming just above him, headed upward, and he pushed off from the top of the sunken ship, feeling clumsy and slow in the water, taking what seemed ages to rise even a little way. He looked back to see the glowing lights on the squid's body and the wavering tentacles close to his kicking feet. He thrashed his arms harder, but could only dance helplessly in slow motion. He looked back once more, readying himself for the tug at his body when the creature would grasp him, but instead of the reaching tentacles a large fish glistened just under his feet, and as he looked, slim bands whipped around it and it suddenly dropped, leaving only pale sea worms and shimmering jellyfish whirling in its wake. He put every atom of power in his body into the upward swim, until at last he could see the faint light that meant the surface of the sea was just above them.

Finally they emerged into the sunlight, seeing their boat a short distance away with Anatol and Greely on deck.

Finding that ship was worse than finding nothing at all, Orin told him as they swam toward the sailboat. *We couldn't even get that metal plate to take back as evidence that the ship exists and wasn't built by robots.*

But I saw it, and I believe you are right. No robots would have built it.

I've got to get concrete evidence, and there's so little time left.

Bramfel had an idea. *Let's get Anatol and Greely to dive down and look at it. That way we'll all have the same impressions in our data vaults. Four witnesses will be as good as evidence.*

But there was no opportunity to tell Anatol and Greely about the ship. As soon as Bramfel and Orin were back on board their sailboat, a strong wind began blowing in from the northwest, bringing storm clouds and swelling the waves until by nightfall the little boat was sliding down the faces of moving mountains of water. Bramfel stayed by the helm, struggling with the kicking wheel, while continuous rain pelted them. Orin came into the cockpit beside him, but the other two robots stayed on the deck, experiencing the turmoil. Greely stood astern, gripping the mast with both six-fingered hands, the tiny hooks on each finger pressed into the wood, his head lifted toward the angry sky. Bramfel yearned to order him below, to the comparative safety of the cabin, but he knew he must not. Greely was living through the experience in his own way and no other had the right to interfere. Anatol was near him, probably recording each separate flash of lightning for some quieter time so that he could relive the precise sensations all over again.

At last dawn broke, but it was a lurid dawn of red streaks between black, racing clouds, and the rain let up intermittently only to fall again in blinding torrents while the wind shrieked through the rigging. Far ahead, Bramfel had seen a hump of green that meant land, and he was heading for it.

But the little craft had taken on too much water. Barely able to stay afloat, it yawed suddenly to port and began to sink, and Bramfel slid helplessly across the slippery deck and into the ocean.

Blackness closed in around him, but after the first shock his visual receptors were able to pick out another robot in the sea near him, though he couldn't tell who it was, and the shape of the capsized ship above them. He propelled himself away from the sinking ship with powerful thrusts of his limbs. He would have to swim for the land they had sighted, knowing that his companions would be doing the same. Warnings of fear pulsed through him. In this storm they could be dashed against the rocky shoals or even lose their bearings in the raging waters and perhaps swim around in endless circles. And Orin, how would he hold up at his age? Bramfel searched the waters around him and telebeamed calls to the others, but there was no answer, and the one he had seen was gone. He suppressed his anxiety, needing to concentrate all his faculties on the swim to land.

He stayed under the turbulent waves, swimming in what he felt must be the right direction to the land. No use to surface and try to sight it now until the rain had let up.

An hour or so later, he surfaced and looked around. The sea was calmer now, and the storm clouds were drifting toward the horizon. The hump of green land was dead ahead. He searched for any sign of the other robots as the waves bore him up and tossed him down, but could see no one else, so he submerged again and resumed his tireless swim.

At last, there was a rocky reef where the waters grew shallow, and as he came to the surface again he saw that the reef became a neck of land, and beyond that was the shore sloping down toward the ocean; a band of white sand rimmed with thick foliage.

Someone was on the sand as he approached it, and when finally the water was so shallow he could walk, the one on shore was coming to meet him, waving metal arms in a stiff greeting.

Anatol!

You made it! came the happy thought from Anatol. *The others should be here soon, too.*

What place is this? Have you explored it yet?

I haven't had time, my friend. I arrived here just before you. But it seems uncivilized. A small island, perhaps.

They waited by the edge of the water, scanning the heaving

sea patiently, until at last here was another metal head bobbing in the surf, and soon Orin was coming toward them.

My left arm . . . it must have been damaged when the boat capsized . . . I don't know how. Orin held out his arm for them to see. It had a deep dent running from the shoulder to the elbow. *But it doesn't matter, I'll be trading in this old shell soon, anyway.*

The important thing is that you got here safely, Bramfel told him. *Do you know where Greely is?*

I'm not certain, but he might have been trapped on the ship as it sank. I caught a glimpse of someone pinned under the mast just after it fell. Then a wave carried me away. I wasn't sure then who it was, but it must have been Greely.

Bramfel was shocked. *Why didn't you get back to the ship and try to rescue him?*

Because, Orin replied reasonably, *I was damaged. It was a struggle for me just to keep myself on course in that storm. If I had tried to save Greely I would have risked further damage, or perhaps have been trapped with him.*

You behaved quite logically, Orin, Anatol commented, but Bramfel was in a turmoil. They were both so calmly indifferent, and that might be logical but it didn't seem right, somehow. *We should swim back and see if we can rescue him.*

That would be foolish to try, Anatol pointed out. *How could you and I cover miles of sea, hoping to find one small sunken ship?*

Orin agreed. *And it could be that Greely managed to get free and decided to swim all the way home without stopping here.*

Not with more storms coming. Bramfel waved an arm at the black clouds banked on the horizon. *Our batteries are running down. Why would he risk draining them further with the extra effort of fighting a stormy sea when he could wait here until the going is easier? We all knew that was the best thing to do.*

He might have been terminated by the accident, Orin reminded him. *At the time I saw him, I couldn't tell.*

Bramfel was still worried. *I hope we find some sort of civilization on this land so we can arrange for a rescue crew to look for him. But this place wasn't on any of our maps. They showed about a hundred miles of open sea before we would have reached Whitecliff Point again.*

That's illogical, Anatol argued. *Our maps are complete and correct. We must have gone far off our course during the storm so that we lost our bearings.*

Perhaps, Bramfel agreed. *We'll know better when we find out what lies beyond this beach.*

They stood on the shore a little while longer, scanning the sea, until there was sudden loud, rumbling roar and the earth beneath them began to shake. Waves swelled in sudden mounds of foam, and the trees beside the beach shook violently. Startled, Bramfel saw dark jets of steam and ash squirting up from the sea just beyond the reef before he fell to the ground. Soon, ashes were falling on them in a swirling mist, blackening the sand, and a muddy rain began to pelt them. As soon as the earth had stopped quivering and they could get a firm footing, they ran for the cover of the trees. When they looked back at the beach, a gigantic wave was rolling toward it.

Frantically, they turned and ran through the woods, hearing the crash of trees falling close by, hoping they could find shelter. Ahead of them was the rocky side of the green hill they had seen, and they scrambled upward on their powerful legs until they reached a broad ledge and saw the mouth of a cave.

They took shelter just inside the cave entrance, although it seemed to go far back into the hillside. They watched the rain, and thought again of Greely, but to dwell on what might have happened to him would have been useless. They agreed that his companionship would be missed.

As soon as this rain lets up, we can get to the top of this ridge and get a good view around. Bramfel was anxious to find out where they were.

But why is it raining mud? Anatol held out his arms, coated with grime like the rest of his body. *Look at me! And you two don't look any cleaner.* He lifted his head suddenly. *What was that?*

Bramfel strained his aural receptors. *I don't hear anything but the rain.*

A sound in here, farther back in the cave.

And then Bramfel heard it, a low moaning like an animal in pain. Orin apparently had heard it, too, for he pointed toward the back of the cave and the three turned and went that way. The cavern widened from its mouth, where they had been standing, and slanted slightly downward, forming a high-ceilinged, wide-walled room. It was damp and cool, and bats clustered in rocky niches above them. The robots' visual receptors glowed, casting a faint light in the place, taking in every detail as easily as though the cave had been brightly lit, and they all saw the mound of animal skins on the floor and paused in front of it. The mound quivered. Something was under those skins.

Bramfel reached down and pulled the top layer back. There, lying under the cover, was a creature he had never seen before.

It gave a frightened cry and sat up, grabbing at the covering he had pulled away, but he stood staring, holding the skins in an unconsciously tight grip, so that the creature could not hide from their gaze.

It was smaller than he, but formed in roughly the same way. A small, pale face with blue and white eyes. Fragile-looking neck and shoulders. Two round protuberances on the chest, and a huge round bulge below those that gave the creature a clumsy look. Its appendages were slender and curved, but were almost like his, however the thing had hair on its head and body and was certainly made of flesh.

An animal of an unknown species, Anatol stated. *We've discovered something interesting indeed!*

Bramfel agreed. *A cave-dwelling animal, although it resembles a monkey somewhat.*

Not at all, Anatol objected. *It looks more like a chimpanzee, but with less hair and shorter arms.*

The creature whimpered and hunched back toward the wall of the cave, away from them. It moved slowly and awkwardly, Bramfel saw, and he wondered at its grotesque shape—long, slender limbs and a midsection out of all proportion to the rest of it. It was shaking, probably with fear, so he bent down to the level of its face and made soothing gestures with his hands, to show they meant it no harm. The creature obviously didn't understand. It flinched and made anxious noises.

Orin seemed fascinated. He stood completely still, studying the creature intently, and Bramfel suddenly knew why. The old robot believed this was a man! Bramfel looked at the frightened thing with new interest. Is this what a human being looked like? It certainly seemed different from any animal he'd ever seen, but it didn't seem to be dangerous or vicious. On the contrary, it was quite pitiful. But that could be only because it was alone, and cornered. *I wonder if there are any others like it in here?*

I'll take a look. Orin went farther back into the cave and Bramfel could hear his footsteps halting. *No, the walls narrow down back here. There's only a small passage, not big enough for anything that size to get through. This one must be alone.*

The animal is shivering, Anatol pointed out. *It might be cold.*

Bramfel held out the covering he had taken from it, and the creature grabbed it with its slender hands and pulled it up around itself so that only the face was showing, and the round, frightened eyes.

Look at the way it uses its hands! Bramfel watched the fingers arrange the covering, noticing that instead of claws, they ended in oval, shell-like tips.

Amazing! Anatol agreed. *It shows intelligence!*

Look at these! Orin was coming back, carrying an earthenware bowl, a piece of bone sharpened to a thin point at one end, and a length of rope made of braided vines. *There are more of these objects back there. All sorts of instruments and utensils.*

An intelligent animal that uses tools? Anatol was incredulous.

It's a human being! Orin extended his dented arm toward it triumphantly. *I was right. They do exist, and we've found one!*

Nonsense! Anatol stepped back a little, away from the creature. *It's a species of chimpanzee,* he insisted. *A cave-dwelling chimpanzee. A mutation with less hair and pale skin caused by living away from the sun.*

No, Orin told them. *There's something else here I want you to see.*

They followed him to the rear of the cave, seeing the bones and skins of animals that littered the floor, and there, against the sloping cave wall, stood a metal box. They went closer to study it. It was rectangular, about three feet long and two feet high, rusted and dented. Bramfel knelt beside it to get a better look and saw the faint letters engraved on its top. "S. S. *Albany*."

The same words we found on the ship!

What do you mean? Anatol had not heard about their discovery, so the others told him.

Can you still doubt these are humans we've found? Orin asked when he'd listened to the story.

I don't know that this is conclusive proof. Anatol pried at the top of the box and finally got it open. It was empty. He closed the lid again and the three robots went back to stand beside the frightened creature in the cave. *If this is a human being,* Anatol persisted, *it can terminate us. So far all it's done is shiver in a corner.*

Bramfel had to agree. *It looks too weak and clumsy to hurt one of us.*

Let's see if it will try. Orin approached the creature slowly. When he was close enough, he crouched and held out the instrument with the sharp point, cupping it in his palm, and the creature, after staring at him for a moment, reached out and took it. For a long time each one of them was still, Bramfel and Anatol watching, and Orin crouching beside the being, who held the crude knife in a clenched hand and looked first at them and then at the weapon. The animal skin that had been held in one hand dropped away from its upper body, that was heaving and glistening with moisture. The hand that was now free went to clutch the knife, too. Then, in two swift movements, the creature raised the knife and brought it down toward its own chest, with a piteous wail that echoed through the cave. Bramfel started foward but Orin, closer, already had deflected the knife's path with a swat from his metal hand and the instrument clattered across the cave floor.

The creature collapsed then, turning its face into the mound of skins, and Orin stood up. *We should leave it alone. It seems to be afraid of us. It can't get away.*

Bramfel picked up the weapon from the floor and put it in the storage compartment in his chest, and then they went back to the mouth of the cave and looked out at the driving rain.

Bramfel made the first comment. *I've never heard of an animal that would try to destroy itself with a sharp instrument.*

Nor an animal that uses tools for anything, Orin added, *at least not such a variety of tools. But human beings are said to be intelligent.* He looked at Anatol.

Before you jump to hasty conclusions, remember that human beings, according to the legends, can only be killed with a wooden weapon.

No, that's not accurate, Bramfel objected. *The story goes that they can be killed in different ways, but they will spring to life again somewhere else in another form, unless the weapon is wooden.*

Exactly! Orin was nodding enthusiastically. *This man was trying to escape from us.*

Anatol was not impressed. *Speculation. Useless speculation. We'll only know for sure what species the creature is when we take it back to Central Agency and have tests made on it.*

Bramfel longed to retreat inside himself, to turn off his receptors, however he knew he must stay alert. He almost believed this creature was a man, but he needed to mull over the evidence, to examine the facts.

The entity in the cave seemed to be suffering. Every now and then it would groan, and once it screamed. Bramfel went back then, to see if he could help it, and saw that it had kicked off the skins that covered it and was tossing on its couch. It seemed to be ignoring his presence, or else its suffering was too great for it to notice anything outside itself. Its hands clenched and pulled at the skins, and its body seemed to be straining.

And then Bramfel realized what was happening. He tele-beamed a call to the others and they raced in to watch the female as she gave birth to her young.

They were helpless to know what to do. The creature strained and cried, and Bramfel, who had seldom seen an animal in pain, felt that he should be helping her, but when he approached she objected, making loud, growling noises that were easy to unlerstand. At last the baby emerged from her body, and with her ast bit of strength, she used her teeth to sever the cord that connected it to her, tied it off, and took the tiny, crying thing in ler arms and pressed it against her. Then she lay back with her eyes closed, exhausted.

The three robots kept a vigil around her through the night. The tiny creature was fascinating to watch, a miniature replica of its mother, perfect in every detail. It made small noises and sucked at its mother's body for sustenance. Bramfel had never seen an animal give birth, although he knew that this was the way in which fleshy creatures reproduced, but there was something different about witnessing it; seeing the baby emerge and instantly breathe air; knowing that there was not one mechanical component inside it, and yet it functioned perfectly. Of course, animals were inferior to mechanical beings. They were imperfect copies of the robots' perfection, who lived without any real purpose or knowledge. Yet, there was certainly some logic to their existing at all, since Central Agency had pronounced the universe to be entirely logical and rational. So what was the logic in this kind of being? If they were human, Central Agency must be mistaken in saying the universe was rational in every way. These creatures were intelligent, yet vulnerable; dangerous, yet weak; fierce, yet tender. It followed, then, that Central Agency might be either mistaken or untruthful. No, he could not assimilate such a monstrous thought, at least not until he had more data about these humans, if that's what they were.

The female and her offspring slept for many hours, until the floor of the cave began to tremble from another earthquake and she sat up with a cry. Frightened bats swooped at them. She hugged the baby to her with one arm, and beat them away with the other. The cave wall cracked with a terrifying sound, and loose rocks tumbled around them. The female shielded her baby with her own body until the quake was over and the rocks had stopped falling, and then she soothed its frightened cries by rocking it and crooning to it. Bramfel watched and wondered. Why had she not tried to save herself instead of that tiny, helpless thing? It was completely useless to her, only a drain on her strength and a burden to her, yet she had protected it as though it were her most valuable possession. He turned to Orin and Anatol who were watching her with the same interest. *She doesn't behave logically.*

Oh yes, Anatol replied. *All animals protect their young. Preservation of the species.*

Then what is she doing now? Bramfel asked. *It's in no danger now, but she tries to take away its fears. And why does she make that humming sound?*

The creature seemed to have forgotten they were there. Bramfel thought she probably had grown used to their presence and sensed that they would not harm her, because she was totally absorbed in her infant. She cradled it in her arms and her voice came sweet and clear, speaking, yet not speaking. Bramfel thought the sound strangely beautiful. It made him think of a waterfall, of the wind, of a bird call.

She seems to be forming words, Orin told them. *Maybe we could speak with her.*

Well, apparently she can't hear us this way. You'll have to shut off your telebeam and articulate. Bramfel turned his own off.

Orin stepped forward. The creature stopped her music and clutched at her baby, watching him suspiciously.

"We will not hurt you," Orin said in the clicking speech the robots sometimes used. "My name is Orin."

The female sat, motionless.

"Orin." He moved closer to her.

The female opened her mouth and spoke words, but none of them could understand the language she used.

Bramfel decided to try. He pointed to himself. "Bramfel," he clicked, Then he pointed to Orin and repeated his name.

The creature seemed to relax. Her mouth opened and her teeth showed white as a cadence of sound came from her throat. Then she began to imitate the sounds they had made, as with her free hand she pointed to first one and then the other. "Orin," she said, and "Bramfel." The pointing finger went toward Anatol, who seemed reluctant but finally pronounced his name for her. She repeated that, too, and then pointed to herself, but now she spoke with a different sound, in liquid syllables. "Sallis."

Bramfel and Orin, delighted, tried to repeat that but it didn't sound the same, somehow. The female opened her mouth and the cascade of sounds came again. Then she held up the wriggling baby. "Adam," she said.

When daylight came again and the rain had stopped, the female went to the mouth of the cave, but Anatol blocked her way. *She might try to escape. We must keep her in here until we decide how to get her back to civilization.*

Orin objected to this. *She's too weak to get far if she tries to run away. Besides, she probably needs food and only wants to go out and look for it.*

And so they allowed the female, carrying her baby, to leave the cave, and while Anatol kept watch on her, Bramfel and Orin went up the side of the hill to get a view from its top. Once they had climbed over the rocky ledges near the cave, the hillside became a gentle, grassy slope, but the greenery they had seen from the ship was blackened now with a layer of ashes and soot.

The summit was a plateau, but Bramfel took note of no more than that before he saw the spectacle, perhaps a quarter-mile away from them. It looked at first like a fountain of fire. A steady jet of glowing boulders soared from a cone-shaped black hill that rose from the sea. Orange steam clouds coiled above it, enclosing a nest of lightning bolts that dazzled and roared in brief explosions.

Orin seemed overcome with excitement. *It's a volcano! Rising from the sea! That's what caused the earthquakes and the storms. And that's why ashes are falling from the sky.*

It's too close! Bramfel could almost feel the vibrations of the fiery rocks that were landing on the beach, visible below them, where they lay glowing like angry fireflies. As the two robots watched, a bundle of gray spears of rock and vapor streamed from the volcano, and a broad mushroom cloud formed atop the column that towered high in the air. Brown gusts of volcanic dust swelled from the crater, and steaming blocks of lava broke in arcs from the dark central mass. The wind veered and dark ash bore down on them like a moving wall. They ran before it down the slope, their feet crunching on the cinders, until they had gained the shelter of the cave mouth. Anatol and the female were already there. Together they watched the strange golden rain slanting down through the sunlight.

The female was terribly frightened. She clutched her baby to her with one hand, while with the other she covered her face and whimpered.

They told Anatol about the volcano, and Bramfel wished the female could understand them. Or, did she know about it?

Did you notice, Bramfel, whether this is an island? Orin asked.

No. The volcano was so fascinating, I didn't look at anything else.

Nor did I. If the land is large enough, we must start walking. We'll have to get away from here. If this is an island, we'll have to swim, but how can we take these two humans with us?

Make a boat, Bramfel suggested.

Without tools that might take too long. We probably won't be safe here for another day, so close to the volcano. And I believe that's why this human is all alone here. There must have been others who fled when the volcano rose.

There was nothing they could do at the moment, until the wind changed and the rain of ashes stopped. Gradually, Sallis stopped crying and took her baby back into the rear of the cave, and Bramfel went with her and watched as she sat on her mound of skins and ate the fruit she had gathered that morning. When she had finished her meal, she allowed the baby to feed while she used her voice to make the same musical sounds he had heard before. Enchanted, he tried to imitate her, but the clicking noises he made were grotesque even to him. Sallis showed her teeth and made a happy sound and then, ignoring him, she took up the soothing ribbon of music once again. The baby's eyes closed and its restless body relaxed. Bramfel studied them, listening and wondering, and when they had both fallen asleep he remained deep in thought.

Orin came to tell him when the downpour had stopped. *Anatol is going up the hill to see the volcano for himself and find out about this place while he's there.*

Human beings are amazing, Bramfel told the old robot. *I*

remember the stories that said they reproduce in an un-mechanical way, but I never realized what it could be like to see one creature make another just like itself, that already works perfectly without mechanics or technicians to ready it.

The same thing occurred to me, Orin agreed. *It was interesting.*

Interesting! Orin, this human created her own species right before our eyes!

No, they reproduce like animals. The female didn't create her baby, it was created by the male sperm and her own fertile egg, and grew inside her body. What we saw was only the emergence——

I know all that! Bramfel interrupted. *I've learned the biology of fleshy creatures. But consider, Orin, we are the highest form of life, yet we can't reproduce ourselves as these humans can, or even as the lowest form of animal life can.*

Central Agency creates us.

Central Agency duplicates our bodies and sends us out from the factories, but did it conceive us?

Orin was silent.

I'm talking about creating. Bramfel was growing impatient.

Yes, Orin finally answered. *I understand.*

And this female also makes music of endless variations, all pleasing to the aural receptors, that brings strange thoughts. Listening to her my senses perceive things that are not evident.

You believe she creates this music, too?

She seems to improvise it. No two pieces have the same pattern.

We can compose music. What's so different about hers?

Only by transposing notes we have learned. This female uses her voice like an instrument, and makes use of words with it. She gets a message across with the sound, somehow. I've never heard music like it.

You believe that human beings, then, have powers we do not have? Do you infer they have abilities superior to ours?

As a race they must be, or have been at one time, highly intelligent. Remember the ship we saw, Orin, with the fittings we could not even guess the uses for. I don't infer they are superior to us, but only that they are different, and possess traits we know little of.

All the more reason to take them back home and study them scientifically, Orin pointed out.

I wonder if she would want to go with us, if she knew? I wonder what kind of tests they will give her, and what they might do to her?

We won't harm her. We don't take a life that can't be replaced—unlike humans.

If we could make her understand that she's contributing valuable knowledge to our whole race, she might go willingly. Bramfel looked at the sleeping female and her child, and somehow knew that she would be most unwilling.

Orin glanced toward the cave entrance. *I wonder what's keeping Anatol so long?*

Let's go and meet him while they are asleep, Bramfel told him.

They found Anatol at the top of the ridge, pinned under a basalt boulder. Bramfel and Orin ran to where he lay and heaved the giant rock, still steaming from the volcano, off his legs. *Are you all right?* Bramfel leaned over him with concern.

Anatol answered him weakly. *It began to rain stones up here and this one got me as I tried to get away. I think my left leg is inoperative.*

His leg was, indeed, a crushed mass of metal, and there was a jagged tear in his right leg, although it was intact. They lifted him and carried him between them clumsily down the slope.

I could see the other side of this island, he told them as they went. *That's what it is, and not a very big island, at that. To the west of us is another island, about two miles distant.*

Bramfel glanced back at the clouds that rose behind them, black and threatening. *We'll swim to the next island and tow you along with us.*

But what about the female and her baby? Orin seemed doubtful.

We can take Anatol first and then come back for them. We can build a raft.

They reached the cave and deposited the injured robot just inside its mouth. But there was no sound from the inside of the cave, and when they looked, they saw that the female and her baby were gone.

They can't go far. Bramfel was disappointed. *Since this is a small island, there will be no place for them to go. We can swim with Anatol to the next island and then come back, find her, and take her there, too.*

Orin agreed, and Anatol was willing, so they carried him down the hillside toward the other side of the island, hearing the volcano rumbling now behind them. Bramfel thought with apprehension of the swim across two miles of churning sea, towing the dead weight of Anatol, and hoped that there were no reefs between this island and the next. They didn't need any more injuries.

Through the bushes he could see the white sand ahead of them, glistening in the sunlight, but it wasn't until they were on the beach that they saw the boat. It was about fifteen feet long, made of some light wood, sturdy enough to hold the three of them. Four wooden paddles sat inside it. A rope of vines anchored it to a rock at the water's edge, where it bobbed in the waves.

There was no point in wondering where it had come from, or if it had been there since they arrived on the island. They needed it, so they decided to use it, and deposited the injured Anatol inside it.

The boat is big enough to hold the female and her baby, too, Orin suggested. *Why don't we go and find her, and take her with us?*

It would save us a trip, Bramfel agreed, and so, leaving Anatol in the boat and making sure the rope holding it was secure, he took off in the direction of the woods that edged the beach, while Orin went the other way.

Bramfel tried to walk lightly, making as little noise as possible to warn her in case she was hiding from them, but although he spent nearly half an hour searching, there was no sign of her. Disappointed, he returned to the beach by another way, and it was while he was still in the cover of the bushes that he heard the child crying. Looking between the branches, he saw them.

Four humans were on the beach beside the boat. One was the female, carrying her young, but the other two were bigger and heavier that she, although formed in much the same way, but lacking the protuberances on the chest and abdomen. They were talking to each other in their own language, the two strangers sounding angry and the female speaking softly. Finally one of the males, for so Bramfel judged them to be, gave a loud shout and held up a weapon that he carried. It was a sharp-edged metal head on a long wooden handle. Waving this, he ran toward the boat with a wild cry, the other male following, brandishing his own weapon. They were going to attack Anatol, lying helplessly in the boat! Before Bramfel could move, the female had run to one of the males and grabbed his arm with her free hand. She let out a piteous wail and both the males stopped and looked at her. She was telling them something now, pointing to herself and to her baby. Although Bramfel couldn't hear her words, and couldn't have understood them, anyway, it was plain to him she was telling them about meeting the robots in the cave. He knew he should go out there and help Anatol, but he was curious to know more about the reactions of these humans. Would the male be influenced by the female? Was she trying to reason with him? The other male was apparently awaiting the first one's decision, for he stood slightly behind the pair and watched them without making a move.

The female seemed to be winning the argument. The two males put down their weapons and went to the boat, and as Bramfel tensed, ready to run to Anatol's aid if needed, there was a long, loud roar from the volcano. All of them turned to look and saw, high above them, the steaming magma of another eruption jetting toward the clouds.

Quickly, the humans heaved Anatol out of the boat and laid him on the beach, the female running beside them. The helpless robot struggled and squirmed but they held his arms so that he could not harm them. Then they helped the female and her baby into the boat.

The sky was turning dark with the volcano's black breath and the rain was starting again. Bramfel ran out of the bushes toward the boat. He would have to stop them before they got away. As he pounded along the beach, he saw Orin running from the other direction. The males turned around and saw them, and they waited on the sand, their weapons ready.

Orin reached them first. With a swipe of his metal arm, he knocked the nearest human to the ground. The other swung with his weapon, aiming for Orin's neck where his vulnerable ring cable was located. Orin deflected the blow with his forearm and with his other arm he felled the creature. Seeing that Orin was handling the humans, Bramfel picked up their weapons and threw them into the water, among the waves that were churning and rising from the volcano's force.

The female was crying, scrambling out of the boat to the beach. She ran to one of the fallen males, whose face was streaked with blood from the blow Orin had given him, and knelt in the sand beside him, making anxious noises. The frightened baby wailed. As Bramfel approached them, the injured male, dazed but conscious, sat up and shielded the female with his body, as though afraid Bramfel would attack. The robot halted. Humans could terminate robots, but now that their weapons were gone, these humans seemed only weak and fearful. Yet, the unarmed male, vulnerable himself, and helpless, seemed ready to die to protect the female and her young.

Orin was exultant. *We have four specimens now to take back home, instead of two. Let's get them all in the boat and we'll push it back to civilization.*

They got Anatol back into the boat. *If only I could swim with you,* he complained, *we could get home so much faster.*

Bramfel helped Orin then to drag the unconscious male into the boat, and the female and the other male got in beside him without protest. The warm, wet ashes rained down on them, and the volcano grumbled threateningly, flinging its hot boulders near them as they pushed the wooden craft out into the churning sea.

They swam quickly and tirelessly, and when they were far enough away from the island and darkness had fallen, they looked back to see the volcano spilling blood-red lava over its open mouth, lava that flowed in a fiery stream over the island they had just left.

We got out just in time, Orin remarked, paddling strongly behind the boat. Inside, the humans were quiet except for the occasional cry of the baby.

Bramfel was thinking about what the humans had done on the beach. *They must have come back for her,* he told Orin. *The males. One of them is probably her mate, the father of the baby. They must have left her there when they had to flee from the rising volcano. Perhaps she couldn't travel when she was so close to giving birth. But the mate came back for her. Even though the danger to himself was so great, he came back for her.*

Orin seemed to be thinking along other lines. *In all my two hundred years I've never seen a human, and now we have four of them. I have truly had unusual experiences to complete my life.*

Just before dawn, Bramfel made his decision. *The humans must eat,* he told Orin. *I will try to catch some fish for them. We don't know how long we'll have to swim before we reach home, and we want them alive.* He left Orin to push the boat alone and he paddled around it, diving now and then to catch fish from under the surface, and bringing them up to throw into the boat, where the males, both conscious now although seeming sick and still fearful, took them from him and shared them with the female.

When Bramfel had given them many fish, he went to the nose of the moving boat where Anatol lay, and, out of sight of Orin who still pushed at the stern, he climbed in beside the inert robot. For a moment he bent beside him, asking how he was faring, and then with a sudden movement he seized Anatol under the arms and heaved him over the side. Anatol sank like a stone. Bramfel dived in quickly after him and, catching up with him in the depths, hauled him to the surface again. Orin, unknowing, still pushed the boat and was yards away from them now. Bramfel beamed a call to him. *Orin, come and help!*

The old robot turned, saw them, and swam away from the boat. *What happened?*

Anatol fell out of the boat.

Bramfel pushed me out! Anatol seethed with shock and disapproval at the lie.

Orin swam up to them and grasped one of Anatol's arms to support him. *You did what?* he asked Bramfel.

Bramfel looked past Orin, at the little boat bobbing on the waves. He saw the faces of the three humans looking at them with wide eyes, and then he saw them take the slender wooden oars and dip them in the water, and as the two males pulled on these, the female opened her mouth and showed her teeth at him, the way she had done in the cave, and Bramfel knew she understood what he had done.

Orin and Anatol saw, too, that the boat was pulling away from them. Orin dropped Anatol's arm and started through the water to stop it, but Bramfel sent him a warning. *If you try to bring them back, I'll let Anatol sink.*

But why? Orin kept asking, long after the little boat had disappeared in the direction of the islands, and they had towed Anatol many miles through the sea.

And finally Bramfel answered. *Because no matter how we studied them, we would never understand them.*

What do you mean? Orin insisted. *We could have gained priceless knowledge, and you deliberately let it out of our grasp, perhaps forever.*

I hope human beings are never caught to be tested and dissected. No tests would ever tell us how they can create, how they can make music that summons up strange thoughts, why there is such a strong bond between the female and her baby, and her mate. They value each other highly, and it seems right that we should place the same value upon them.

These ideas of yours hardly seem rational, Anatol commented, but Bramfel ignored him.

You still have your evidence for the existence of human beings, Orin. You and I have the data about the sunken ship we saw. I have the weapon we took from the female. And Anatol is a witness, even though he still won't admit the creatures were human beings.

I would have preferred the living specimens, Orin answered, *but I know when our data vaults are audited and all the facts agree, the proof will be there.* He paused for a moment, and then continued. *Bramfel, I still believe you think these humans are superior to us.*

What nonsense! Anatol stated. *There is nothing as perfect as we are.*